A TALE OF
TWO CITIES

First published in 2002 by Usborne Publishing Ltd,
Usborne House, 83-85 Saffron Hill,
London EC1N 8RT, England.
www.usborne.com

A catalogue record for this title is available
from the British Library.

ISBN 07460 5313 4

Printed in Great Britain

Series editors: Jane Chisholm and Rosie Dickins
Designed by Brian Voakes
Series designer: Mary Cartwright
Cover: guillotine © Dave Bartruff/CORBIS
background © Digital Vision

A TALE OF
TWO CITIES

from the story by **Charles Dickens**
retold by his Great-Great-Great Granddaughter
Lucinda Dickens Hawksley

Illustrated by Bob Harvey

Contents

About A Tale of Two Cities

This gripping story of heroism and self-sacrifice was written by one of the most famous authors of the 19th century, Charles Dickens. *A Tale of Two Cities* was his twelfth novel and, by the time it appeared in 1859, he was already a popular and successful writer. The idea for the plot had come to Dickens in 1857, but he didn't start writing the novel until two years later. By this time he had it well worked out in his head, and it took him just a year to complete.

A Tale of Two Cities is set against the dramatic backdrop of the French Revolution of 1789. Dickens wanted to write accurately about the revolution, so he did a lot of research into French history. He was also greatly influenced by the writings of Thomas Carlyle, a historian whom he much admired. Like Carlyle, Dickens could see parallels between the awful poverty in 18th-century France that had led to the revolution, and the problems of 19th-century Britain.

In Dickens's time, the gap between the rich and the poor in Britain was enormous. People starved on the streets of large cities every day, while the manufacturers and aristocrats got richer and richer.

Social discontent was growing; many were starting to question why some people seemed to have it all, and so many others had nothing and had to watch their children die in poverty.

As well as being a writer, Dickens was very concerned with social issues. Many of his novels address social problems; he deliberately tried to make people look at the truth about what was happening in their world, and sometimes persuaded them to change things. From letters Dickens wrote to friends in the late 1850s, we know that he believed Britain was in great danger of ending up like 18th-century France. *A Tale of Two Cities* was not just a story – it was a warning to the upper classes that working-class people might one day fight back, and that Britain was in danger of falling into revolution.

Yet, despite these fears, throughout the novel Dickens praises England: all those who flee from the revolution in France are guaranteed safety there. Dickens adored London; he knew the city intimately and, when he couldn't sleep, he would spend whole nights walking the streets and discovering new areas. In this novel, London is depicted as a haven for all those who have been persecuted.

A Tale of Two Cities was published in weekly parts in the magazine Dickens edited, *All The Year Round*. This way of publishing weekly episodes was the Victorian equivalent of a TV soap opera; people would line up to buy their copies, eager to find out what had happened in the story that week. Some people would also write letters to the author, begging him not to allow popular characters to die, or trying to find out in advance what fate befell a particularly nasty criminal.

A Tale of Two Cities has had a lasting influence, helping to shape the way many people think of the French Revolution. The terrible scenes Dickens describes, of the trials and executions by Guillotine in Paris, are memorable images. Yet the novel transcends its historical context: the individuals may be caught up in terrifying historic events, but they triumph through love, heroism and self-sacrifice – personal virtues which we can still admire today.

Character List

Dr. Alexandre Manette: A French doctor jailed for eighteen years in the Bastille. Father of Lucie.

Lucie Manette/Darnay: Daughter of Dr. Manette. She marries Charles Darnay.

Charles Saint Evrémonde/Darnay: Nephew of the Marquis Saint Evrémonde and husband of Lucie. He changes his name to Darnay when he renounces his family.

Little Lucie: Charles and Lucie's daughter.

Miss Pross: Lucie's former nurse, now her companion.

Solomon Pross/John Barsad: Miss Pross's younger brother. He calls himself John Barsad when working as an English spy.

Roger Cly: An English spy.

Jarvis Lorry: An employee of Tellson's Bank and a friend of the Manettes.

Jerry Cruncher: A porter at Tellson's Bank. He sometimes works as a "resurrection man", stealing dead bodies for surgeons.

Young Jerry: Jerry Cruncher's son.

C.J. Stryver: An English lawyer who defends Charles when he is tried at the Old Bailey.

Sydney Carton: Stryver's assistant.

Marquis Saint Evrémonde: A French aristocrat and Charles's uncle.

Ernest Defarge: A former servant of Dr. Manette, now a wineshop owner. A leading Revolutionary.

Madame Therese Defarge: Defarge's wife and an important Revolutionary.

The Vengeance: A Revolutionary friend of Madame Defarge.

Jacques: A name used by several Revolutionaries to conceal their true identies.

The Era

It was the best of times, it was the worst of times. A time when everything seemed possible – and nothing seemed possible. An age of confusion.

England was ruled by a king with a large jaw and a queen with a plain face. France was ruled by a king with a large jaw and a queen with a pretty face. None of them seemed to know, or care, about the difficult lives of their people.

Although many of their subjects lived in terrible poverty, both kings were happy. They believed their people loved them, purely because they were kings. They felt safe. Even though they took no time to care about their people in return.

It was 1775. A time when America was tired of being ruled by England, a country so far away, and was starting to ask for independence. The king and government of England didn't really take this seriously. They thought things would always remain the same. They couldn't see the huge changes that were coming.

In France, the king was equally blind to the truth and he allowed the church far too much bullying power. One day a group of monks executed a young man because he hadn't knelt down when they passed

– even though he'd been standing so far away he might not have seen them. The church had great power and the man was too poor to have any. The king said nothing.

The young man's death added fuel to a fire that was already burning inside the ordinary people of France: woodsmen, farmers, people who worked for their living and starved when food was scarce. Inside them, resentment was growing.

In England, people were terrorized by a different fear: daring burglaries were taking place – it seemed everywhere. Armed thieves robbed houses all over London, despite the efforts of the law. Highwaymen controlled the roads. No one was safe. Even the Lord Mayor of London himself was held up by a highwayman and stripped of all his possessions!

The government of England was desperate to put an end to the thieving, and so scores of people were put to death – many of them innocent. If the king ordered an end to crime, someone must pay the penalty. So the hangman was always busy: one day he'd execute a terrible murderer, the next day a petty thief. It was just his job.

That was how things were in 1775. The ordinary people worked and worked for smaller and smaller rewards, getting ever poorer and hungrier – and now they were growing angry. Meanwhile, their kings and queens continued in careless ignorance, not knowing that a terrible chapter of history was about to begin.

Shadows in the Night

One Friday night in late November, Mr. Jarvis Lorry was walking along the road that led from London to Dover. He and two other men had paid to travel in the Dover mailcoach. But they were walking in front of it instead. The hill was so steep the horses couldn't pull the coach with them inside it. The passengers were not pleased: it was a wet, muddy road and it was after eleven o'clock at night.

The hill was called Shooters Hill – so named because there were so many highwaymen nearby.

13

Understandably, Mr. Jarvis Lorry and his two fellow passengers were more than a little apprehensive. There was a cold mist lurking, hanging over everything in the road, blocking out the light of the moon so that it was hard even to make out the bright lights on the coach.

The coach itself was protected by a guard with guns, but he and the driver were still worried. After all, what good was one armed guard against two or more armed highwaymen?

In 1775, no one trusted strangers. The guard suspected the passengers, the passengers suspected one another and the guard, and the coachman suspected everyone. The three passengers were walking as close to the coach as possible, terrified that every sound or movement in the undergrowth might be a highwayman about to attack.

Finally the horses reached the top of the hill. The passengers were starting to climb back into the coach when they were disturbed by the unmistakable sound of hooves.

The guard cocked his blunderbuss, ready to shoot at the first sign of trouble. The three passengers stopped still, not daring to move in case the guard mistook them for a highwayman's mate. They could feel their hearts beating so loud they were sure the others could hear. The galloping horse came closer and closer.

Suddenly the guard shouted out, "You there! Stop, or I shall fire!"

The horse stopped. A deep, chilling voice rose out of the mist, "Is that the Dover mailcoach?"

"Never you mind," the guard retorted. "Who are you?"

"Is that the Dover mail? I'm looking for one of the passengers."

"Who?"

"Mr. Jarvis Lorry."

The guard looked around. Jarvis made a gesture to show it was his name that had been spoken. The others eyed him distrustfully.

"Keep where you are," the guard called to the stranger.

"Is that Jerry?" Jarvis said, nervously.

"Yes, Mr. Lorry."

Jarvis sighed with relief. "What's the matter?" he asked.

"I've brought you a message from the bank."

"I know this man," Jarvis told the guard. "Please allow him to come and give me the message."

"Come on foot," barked the guard, "and let me see your hands up high, with no weapon in them."

Jerry stepped forward and handed a note to Jarvis, who explained, "It's from Tellson's Bank in London, my place of work. I'm going to Paris on business and Jerry has brought me a note that must be read before I set off."

Grumpily, the guard told him to be quick about it. Jarvis opened the note; it contained just five words: "Wait at Dover for Mam'selle." That was all.

He smiled and spoke to Jerry, "Thank you, and tell the bank my answer is 'Recalled to life'. When they hear those words, they'll know it was me who received the letter and no one else. Go carefully, Jerry. Goodnight."

At this, Jarvis climbed into the coach. His two fellow passengers were already inside and had hastily hidden their watches and purses inside their boots. Neither trusted this stranger who received midnight messages from deep-voiced horsemen and gave such mysterious replies. Both men pretended to be asleep, nervous of being drawn into conversation with him.

The coach continued on its way. As it drew further away from London, the guard relaxed his tight hold on his blunderbuss, relying solely on the two smaller pistols he wore on his belt.

"Tom," he called softly to the coachman.

"Yes?"

"Did you hear the message?"

"I did."

"What did you make of it?"

"Nothing at all."

"I couldn't understand it either," muttered the guard.

All night long, both men mulled over the strange expression, "recalled to life". So did Jerry on his dark, lonely ride back to the city of London.

Jerry rode back at a much slower pace. He stopped regularly at ale-houses, slaking his thirst at every one. Yet he talked to no one while he drank, keeping his hat pulled down well over his eyes.

Jerry's eyes were dark and very close together, which gave him a sinister, shifty expression. His head was balding, but the hair he still possessed looked like stiff, black wires sticking straight up from his scalp. His face was obscured by a thick scarf which he moved only to allow himself to drink, quickly covering his face as soon as he'd taken a gulp. While he drank, he repeated "recalled to life" again and again, trying to make sense of it.

Eventually, he mounted his horse a final time and trotted back to Tellson's Bank. Here he was to deliver Jarvis's message to the night watchman, who'd pass it on to the anonymous authorities within the walls of that great bank. His horse, more afraid of the night than her rider seemed to be, shied at every unexpected shadow that loomed up out of the darkness.

As the horse shied and stopped and Jerry coaxed her on, the Dover Mail was continuing on its equally bumpy way. All three passengers inside slept, dreamed and brooded on their own inner secrets. Jarvis, half-asleep, wandered in his mind through the underground vaults of Tellson's – all the time aware that he was on his way to dig somebody out of a grave.

In his mind he could see the man. He was about forty-five years old, with prematurely white hair. His face mutated constantly in Jarvis's mind, sometimes cowed, sometimes proud, at times stubborn, at other times submissive. Images ran through his mind: the face was gaunt, the cheeks sunken, skin the shade of death. The man's face was beaten, his body emaciated, he was a worn, wasted figure... But Jarvis was on his way to set this man free. In his head he held conversations with the man, whose answers were always the same.

"You've been buried how long?"

"Almost eighteen years."

"Had you abandoned all hope of ever being recovered?"

"Yes, long ago."

A jerk of the coach woke Jarvis with a start. He lowered the window and looked out at the rising sun. The night shadows had disappeared. Though the earth was cold and wet, the sky was clear and the sun rose bright, placid and beautiful.

"To be buried alive for eighteen years!" he said, looking up at the sun. "Imagine it, eighteen years!"

A Discovery

By the time the coach reached Dover, Jarvis was the only passenger left. The straw-covered floor had become damp and dirty, and smelled more like a dog kennel than a gentleman's carriage. Jarvis was more than happy to leave it for the comfort of the Royal George Hotel.

After making inquiries, he discovered that the next day's boat for Calais would leave at two o'clock in the afternoon. In the meantime, Jarvis requested a bedroom and a barber to shave him. He was led to a room with a fine fire and was promised a barber as soon as possible.

Jarvis eventually emerged from the room as a smart, slim, well-dressed man of about sixty, with kindly, bright eyes and a carefully arranged wig.

At breakfast, he asked a servant to arrange accommodation for a young woman who would be arriving at the hotel that day, and to let him know when she came.

After eating, he walked along the beach. At that time, Dover was a place where invalids were brought to bathe in the "healing" waters of the sea. It was also a popular haunt for smugglers. Jarvis stayed on the beach all day, watching people come and go.

After dark, he sat in the hotel staring at the fire – and all the time his mind was busy digging, digging, digging. At last he heard wheels rattling into the courtyard. A few minutes later, it was announced that Miss Manette had arrived from London and had asked to see him. Apprehensively the banker made his way to meet her.

Lucie Manette was a pretty girl of about seventeen, small and slight, with golden hair and inquiring blue eyes. Jarvis remembered the small child he'd held in his arms for the long, cold journey across the English Channel so many years before.

"I received a letter from the bank," she began, "telling me a discovery had been made regarding the property of my poor, dead father, and that a man from your bank would be going to Paris. Is that you?"

"Yes, miss."

"Please could I travel with you? I was told a message would be sent to you from the bank, and that you had more information for me."

"I received the message and am very happy to

accompany you," replied Jarvis. "As for the information, it's not easy..." He stopped, awkwardly.

Lucie interrupted, "Excuse me, but have we met before?"

But Jarvis rushed on. "I have a story to tell you. A story of one of our customers, a French doctor and scientist, a man who lived in Beauvais..."

"Like my father," she observed.

"Yes, just like your father. Like Dr. Manette, this gentleman was well known in Paris. At that time I had been in Paris for twenty years."

"When was this?"

"About twenty years ago, miss. When he married an English lady..."

"But this is my father's story!" she interrupted him again. "When I was left an orphan, it was you who brought me back to England. I'm sure it was you."

Mr. Lorry nodded. Miss Manette had been left a ward of Tellson's Bank, he explained briskly – not without a pang of regret that he had not done more to befriend his friend's child.

"So far, miss, as you've realized, this was the story of your father's life. Now comes the difference: if your father had not died..." he stopped as she started in alarm and caught his wrist with both hands. "As I was saying, if your father had not died, if he had instead been spirited away to prison, if it had been impossible to know where he'd been taken or why, if his wife – before her death – had petitioned the king and queen, the court and the clergy all in vain... then it would be the story of your father."

Piece by piece the explanation emerged in Jarvis's frustratingly slow, ponderous way… that the doctor's wife had been pregnant – that she'd decided before the child was born it should know nothing of the agonies she'd suffered when her husband disappeared – that the child should believe its father to be dead. A few months after the doctor's disappearance, she had given birth to their daughter. That baby was Lucie Manette.

"Your mother never stopped searching for your father. When she died, you were only two. She wanted you to grow up happy, not knowing of your father's uncertain fate." Jarvis paused, then continued gently, "The discovery we've made is not of any money or possessions, as you were led to believe. Your father has been found! He is alive, though in what circumstances or condition it's impossible to say. He's been taken to the house of an old servant who lives in Paris. We're going there, you and I, to identify him and to bring him to England. We're going to restore him to life."

Lucie listened silently, while Jarvis continued to speak. He told her they must find her father and bring him to England as fast as possible. France was in turmoil; these were dangerous times. There would be no time for questions. They were to tell people merely that they were there on business for the bank.

While he was talking, Lucie fainted. Help appeared in the form of a large, wild-looking woman, with florid skin and thick, red hair. She rushed up to Lucie, pushing Jarvis out of the way with such force that she sent the slightly built man flying back against the wall.

This was Miss Pross, at one-time Lucie's nanny and now her devoted companion. She was looking at Jarvis with contempt. Jarvis hazarded to ask if she would accompany them to France. Her reply was curt.

"How likely is that?" she snorted. "If the Good Lord intended me to cross salt water, I wouldn't have been born on an island!"

This was hard to dispute. Mr. Lorry apologized and quickly left the room.

A Visit to Paris

In Saint Antoine, a rundown region of Paris, a large cask of wine had fallen off a cart and broken in the street. Red wine had splashed all over the paving stones. At once, people stopped whatever they were doing and rushed to lap up the liquid from the grooves and crevices of the well-worn stones.

Every pool of wine was surrounded by a group of emaciated men, women and children, jostling one another. People appeared with small mugs to scoop it up, others made cups of their hands, drinking quickly before the precious liquid disappeared through the cracks between their fingers. Others untied rags from their hair or pulled the shirts off their backs, using them to soak it up, and still more

24

grabbed sodden pieces of smashed wood floating in the puddles – these rags and planks were sucked dry of wine, mud and whatever grime had gathered in the pools. All along the street the sound of gulping, lapping and laughter could be heard.

When the last drop of wine had been licked, life suddenly reverted to normal. Barefoot children, skinny babies, ragged men and scrawny women returned to their tasks, their hands, faces and clothes stained red with wine, as though with blood.

Now the excitement had passed, misery started to return. Their brief good fortune had made people forget the ever-present cold and the continual threat of sickness and hunger – grinding them down and spreading through their bones. The baker's shop had only a few small loaves of bad bread for sale. The butcher sold scraggy sausages made from minced carcasses of dead dogs, rats and other animals from the streets.

A wine shop stood at the corner of the street. The shop's owner, Monsieur Defarge, had stood outside it watching the struggle for the spilled wine. He wasn't bothered about the accident; it cost him nothing. The carters who had dropped the cask would pay for it, not him. He liked the fact that hungry people were being given sustenance for free.

Defarge was a bull-necked, tough-looking man of about thirty. Dark-haired, with friendly dark eyes, but not someone to be crossed. Once he took up a cause he would stop at nothing to see it through to the end. Madame Defarge, his wife, was sitting behind the counter. She was a sturdy, strong-looking woman. She always seemed to look through people rather than at them – and she never missed a thing. In front of Madame Defarge was her knitting, which she had put down briefly to pick at her teeth with a toothpick. As her husband came in she gave a little cough, to indicate they had new customers.

Defarge noticed an elderly man and young woman seated in the corner, but pretended not to have seen them. He began chatting to three men drinking at the bar. Anyone listening would have noticed something curious: all the men were named Jacques. Suddenly the three men stood up, paid for their wine and made to leave the shop. Defarge accompanied them to the door, telling them how to find the room they wanted to rent from him – although no room had been mentioned in their conversation. He pointed out a narrow doorway across the courtyard, and left them to make their way to it.

Jarvis got up from the corner where he'd been sitting with Lucie and muttered something to Defarge, who listened intently, nodded and went out. Then Jarvis beckoned to Lucie, and they too left the shop. They crossed the courtyard to the narrow doorway, where Defarge was waiting for them. As they reached him, he took Lucie's hand and kissed it with affection, greeting her as the daughter of his old master. Then he led them inside and up some stairs.

"Has he changed very much?" whispered Jarvis.

There was a nod and Jarvis shuddered.

At the top of the staircase was a door. The three Jacques were standing in front of it, peering through a peephole. Defarge asked them to leave and they glided away, silently, without looking around.

"Do you treat Dr. Manette like a freak show?" demanded Jarvis.

"I show a few people, men who will benefit from seeing him," was all Defarge would answer. "They haven't done him any harm." Then he knocked loudly on the door, asked Jarvis and Lucie to stand well back, and unlocked it.

The room, which had originally been a storeroom, was dark, with just one small window. In the gloom, with his back towards the door, sat a white-haired man on a low bench. He was absorbed in his work, busily making shoes.

"Good day," said Defarge to the white head bent low over the shoemaking bench.

"Good day," was the reply. The voice was faint and dull.

"Still hard at work I see."

This time the cobbler looked up, but showed no sign of recognition. "Yes, I'm still working," he said and bent his head again.

Jarvis and Lucie noticed his haggard, dead-looking eyes, but he still hadn't spotted them in the doorway. He seemed enclosed in another, tiny world with no space for other people. They heard the dreadful faintness of his voice, a sunken, depressed, mere echo of a voice, the sort one would expect from a dying man. Defarge opened the door a little further, and the sunlight gave Lucie and Jarvis a proper view of the former prisoner.

He sat with an unfinished shoe upon his lap, basic tools and scraps of leather covering the workbench in front of him. His white hair and beard were confused and disordered, as if they had been trimmed with a blunt knife. His face was hollow and his eyes shockingly bright, as though they saw things other people could not. His eyes were naturally large anyway, but the thinness of his face made them look frighteningly so. He wore clothes that had been fashionable eighteen years before. His shirt was now little more than yellowed rags lying open at the throat. Beneath the material, his body was withered and worn. He and his clothes were so faded from years of confinement that Jarvis found it difficult to tell where the clothes ended and the skin began. All had become one dull shade of parchment yellow.

When his eyes had adjusted to the light, the cobbler returned to work, still without noticing the two figures at the door. Defarge motioned to Jarvis to come forward, which he did, treading silently. It was several minutes before the cobbler noticed Jarvis. He didn't seem surprised by the intrusion, but nor did he recognize him.

"You have a visitor," said Defarge. "A gentleman who wants to see what you're making."

Jarvis was handed the shoe and pretended to

examine it before commenting casually, "Please monsieur, what kind of shoe is this and what's the maker's name?"

"It's a lady's shoe, apparently the latest fashion. I've never seen the fashion, but somebody brought me a pattern to work from." For the first time the voice took on a note of pride.

"And the maker's name?" asked Jarvis again, gently.

The cobbler showed signs of anxiety and answered, "105 North Tower."

"Is that all?"

"Yes, 105 North Tower is the maker's name." He returned to work, as though conversation exhausted him.

Jarvis persevered, "You're not a shoemaker by trade?"

"No. I learned it, I taught myself, I asked permission to..." Here, he seemed to fade away. At last he continued, "... I asked permission to teach myself, I needed something to do. It was finally agreed, and I've made shoes ever since." He held out his hand for the shoe.

Jarvis looked into his face and said, "Dr. Manette, don't you remember me?"

The shoe fell to the ground.

"Dr. Manette," Jarvis indicated Defarge, "don't you remember this man? Look at him. Look at me! Can't you recognize us?"

He looked at them, but any recognition was soon replaced by a misty look, as though he were slowly shutting down inside.

Meanwhile Lucie had been silently sidling along the wall, desperate for a proper look at her father. All her life she'd thought him dead, but here he was – though little more than a ghost. Jarvis and Defarge moved away to talk.

"Do you recognize him?" whispered Defarge.

"Yes, for an instant I could see the man he once was."

Unnoticed by anyone, Lucie was edging nearer. She knelt down by Dr. Manette's feet and waited. After a while, he needed a new tool. Looking around for it, he noticed the skirt of Lucie's dress. The sight jolted him. It was an elegant, expensive material, not the kind of thing he was used to seeing in his cell. Slowly he raised his eyes and stared directly into her face. He looked afraid and tried to speak, but no sound came out.

He began struggling for breath and at last whimpered, "What is this?" Deep in his disturbed mind a picture was forming, a picture of his wife, who had looked so like her daughter.

Crying, Lucie looked directly at him. Then she took one of his hands in her own.

"You're not the jailer's daughter?" he asked.

"No!"

"Then who are you?"

Lucie let go of his hand and sat beside him on the

bench. He laid down his tools and reached up to a scrap of folded rag strung around his neck. He unfolded the rag slowly. Inside were a few long, golden hairs. He took up one of Lucie's long blonde curls and looked at the two, side by side. They were identical. He turned her head towards the light to look at her properly and, for the first time, talked clearly about his past.

"She held me that evening, when I told her I'd been called out. She was frightened for me, though stupidly I had no fear. When I was brought to the North Tower, they found these hairs on my sleeve. They were going to take them away, but I asked them to give them to me. I can still remember what I said to my jailers: 'Please leave me those. They can never help me to escape in body, but they may help me escape in spirit'."

Lucie started to speak but the sound of her voice made him cry, as though wounded. He wrapped the hairs back up in his rag and turned away.

"You can't be her, you're too young. Who are you?"

Lucie told him gently who she was. That she'd come from England to find him, that she wanted to take him back there to live with her, where he could be safe. He took hold of her and held her close, hugging the child he'd so often dreamed about but never known.

Jarvis left to arrange for a carriage, so they could leave the cell-like garret as soon as night fell. As they descended the stairs, Dr. Manette looked around him in surprise. He had no recollection of having left the North Tower, or of being brought here. When they reached the courtyard, his body stiffened with fear, expecting barred gates, soldiers, jailers, but there were none – only a carriage. As they were leaving, Dr. Manette suddenly called out for his shoemaking tools. Madame Defarge, who was leaning against the gatepost, went to fetch them. Then she returned to her knitting.

The carriage passed through the lamp-lit streets of Paris, clattering over cobblestones, past brilliantly lit shops, brightly dressed crowds of people, illuminated coffee houses and raucous concert halls. Eventually they reached one of the city gates, where a soldier stepped out of the guardhouse and demanded their papers. Jarvis handed them over and, after a brief word with the soldier, they were free to go.

Five Years Later

Tellson's Bank, at Temple Bar in London, was an old-fashioned place, even in 1780. It was very small, very dark, very ugly and very uncomfortable. In tiny, cramped work spaces, the elderly clerks gravely continued with the business they'd been doing since they were very young men. The bank was an institution that never seemed to change.

A regular fixture outside Tellson's was Jerry Cruncher, the bank's odd-job man and messenger. During banking hours he never left his post outside the door unless sent on an errand, at which time his son would stand in his place.

Early one windy March morning in 1780, Jerry was at home in Whitefriars, a rundown area of London. Jerry's apartment was small and cramped, though his wife kept it as clean as she could. This morning she had made breakfast, laid the table and was praying while her son and husband were sleeping. Mrs. Cruncher was a very religious woman.

When Jerry woke and heard her prayers, he reached out of bed and threw one of his boots at her. He hated his wife's religious ways and accused her of "plotting against him" in her prayers. The boot left spatters of mud over the clean floor. It always amazed their son, young Jerry, that his father could come home with clean boots after a day at the bank, and yet the next morning those same boots would be covered in mud.

Jerry looked red-eyed and grim, as though he'd been up all night instead of sleeping in his bed. He ate his breakfast like a starved animal, growling obscenities from time to time at his downtrodden wife. Then he smoothed his hair, put on his work clothes and left for the bank, taking young Jerry with him. By a quarter to nine he was established on his stool outside the bank, greeting the elderly clerks (and they all seemed to be elderly) as they entered.

Shortly after the start of business, Jerry was dispatched on an errand. His son took up his place on the stool and picked up a straw his father had been idly running through his fingers. It was stained a brownish-red, like dried blood.

"His fingers are always stained red," young Jerry thought to himself, not for the first time. "Where does it come from?"

Jerry's errand was to give a note to Jarvis Lorry, who was taking part in a trial at the Old Bailey, the most famous criminal court in London. He had been told to remain in court until Mr. Lorry wanted him. Jerry asked what kind of trial was taking place that day. "Treason," was the clerk's reply. Jerry's face paled. He knew the fate of a person found guilty of treason was to be "quartered", an extremely barbaric and agonizing punishment where a man was hanged and then cut into pieces.

Familiar with the many confusing doorways and entrances of the Old Bailey, Jerry quickly found the one he needed and squeezed his way into the tightly packed court. It seemed all of London had come to see the trial. Jarvis was sitting with several bewigged barristers. Jerry watched him with interest, wondering how Mr. Lorry could figure in a treason case.

When the prisoner was brought into the dock, the whole court seemed to breathe together like one enormous baying animal. People were climbing onto one another's shoulders to get a look at him. The prisoner, Charles Darnay, was a tall, good-looking man of about twenty-five, with a suntanned face and dark eyes. He was dressed simply, with his long, dark hair tied back from his face. But by the quality of his clothes, Jerry could tell he was a gentleman. If you had looked closely into his eyes, you might have guessed that he was terrified inside, but he hid it well.

On the previous day, the prisoner had pleaded "not guilty" to the charge: that of being a traitor who had assisted the French in their wars against

England. Despite his plea, barely anyone in the court believed him to be innocent. In their minds, he was already a dismembered, dead man.

There were those, however, who would not give up on him. These included his lawyer, Mr. Stryver, a stout, red-faced man, who looked much older than his thirty or so years, and Lucie Manette and her father, who sat silently at the edge of the courtroom.

Dr. Manette now looked like a happy, handsome, middle-aged man – though from time to time, the abused shoemaker could still be seen in his face.

Jerry asked the man next to him who they were.

"Witnesses," was the reply.

"For which side?" asked Jerry.

"The prosecution."

The Trial

Charles Darnay had been observed voyaging regularly between France and England, and had reputedly been seen passing over secret papers. He didn't deny he made the journey frequently. But, although he insisted he wasn't a spy, he could give "no honest account" of what took him across the English Channel so often.

The court was told of a witness, a so-called former friend of Darnay's, who would testify against him. A second witness had also been found, a one-time servant of the prisoner's. The prosecuting Attorney-General spent a great deal of time praising these witnesses as honest, respectable men. The case against Charles was growing more serious every minute.

John Barsad, the first witness, appeared in a courtroom that was fast approaching fever pitch. The Attorney-General asked him several questions, all designed to make him appear a model citizen – though strangely, when he was cross-examined by Mr. Stryver, Barsad seemed rather less trustworthy. Mr. Stryver suggested he was a spy for the Old Bailey and had been paid to accuse Darnay. Barsad denied it hotly, claiming his only motive was patriotism.

The next witness was Roger Cly, who had been Charles Darnay's servant for four years. (Though it later emerged Charles had only hired him after he had begged him for work.) Mr. Stryver also revealed Cly had known Barsad for eight years, twice as long as he'd known Charles. Cly protested that this was entirely coincidence and his accusation was also motivated purely by patriotism.

Then Jarvis was called to the witness box. He admitted that he had met Charles Darnay on board a ship from Calais, when returning to England with the Manettes. That was all he could tell the court.

Lucie Manette was called to the witness box next. She was obviously distressed.

"When the gentleman came on board..." she began.

"Do you mean the prisoner?" snapped the judge.

"Yes, my lord."

"Then say it!"

"When the prisoner came on board, he noticed my father was very ill. He helped me construct a bed to shelter him from the wind and rain. He was very kind."

"Had he come on board alone?"

"No... there were two French gentlemen with him."

"Did they pass any papers between them?"

"They had some papers, but I didn't read them."

"What did the prisoner talk about with you?"

"He was very kind... I hope I'm not going to repay him by doing him harm today." At this, she burst into tears.

"Miss Manette, as you know, you are under oath to tell the truth. I think the whole court, not just the prisoner, understands you're not intending to do him any harm, but you must tell us exactly what was said."

"He told me his business was of a difficult nature, it might get people into trouble, so he was using an assumed name." That was all she knew – but it seemed to her to be enough to condemn the prisoner in the eyes of the Old Bailey.

The Attorney-General then began to defame the prisoner's character further, playing upon the evidence Lucie had so unwillingly given.

Another witness was called, a man who claimed to have seen Charles meeting another "well-known" spy. Mr. Stryver questioned the witness, but he had little to go on. Until now his assistant, Sydney Carton, appeared to have been taking little interest in the trial. But Sydney suddenly seemed to shake himself. He passed a note to Stryver, who read it with interest, then changed his line of questioning.

"You say again that you're sure it was the prisoner you saw that night?"

"Quite sure."

"Have you never seen anyone else who looks like the prisoner? Couldn't it have been someone else?"

"Never. I don't think I could have been mistaken."

"Then look over there at my learned friend…" The entire court room looked at Sydney. "Don't you think he and the prisoner are very similar?"

A hush fell over the Old Bailey. For the first time,

everyone noticed that the prisoner and Sydney Carton looked astonishingly like one another – except that the prisoner looked far more respectable. The witness agreed, reluctantly, that they were indeed very alike.

"Are you still certain it was Charles

Darnay you saw that one night so long ago? Couldn't it have been someone who looked like him?"

The witness was forced to admit he couldn't be certain. The case was turning.

Like a lion waking from sleep, Mr. Stryver returned to the previous witnesses, decrying them as hired spies and forgers of evidence, who had falsely trapped and accused his client. Charles made regular journeys between France and England because his family was French and he had family business to attend to. It was as simple as that.

The Attorney-General then came back into play and turned everything around yet again, painting Charles as more devious than ever, and Cly and Barsad as maligned patriots. Jerry Cruncher, watching from the gallery, became more confused with each step.

Sydney was once again staring at the ceiling – though it must be said that when Lucie Manette started to swoon in her anxiety for the prisoner, Sydney was the first to notice. He saw her head drop even before her father did, and it was Sydney who called to the nearest officer to help her out of court.

Dr. Manette was also greatly agitated by the trial, reminded as he was of his own imprisonment. But he sat in the court resolutely, needing to hear the jury's decision. It was a long time in coming: the jury asked permission to retire and discuss the case. When most people had left the court, Jarvis beckoned to Jerry.

"Go and eat, but don't go far – you'll need to take the verdict back to the bank as soon as it's given."

Relieved, Jerry left to seek out the nearest pub.

Sydney was talking to Charles. "What d'you expect from the jury, Mr. Darnay?" he asked.

"The worst," Charles conceded.

"That's the wisest thing to expect – though I think their withdrawing is a good sign." Then he turned and left abruptly.

An hour and a half later, Jerry returned to the Old Bailey to find Jarvis searching for him.

"Jerry! Here, quick!" Written on the paper Jarvis handed over was a single word: "ACQUITTED."

Congratulations

As the last of the spectators left the court, the Manettes, Jarvis and Mr. Stryver gathered around to congratulate Charles. Stryver was very pleased with himself and was happily blowing his own trumpet. Dr. Manette, however, was looking tired and nervous. Jarvis and Lucie were anxious to get him away from the Old Bailey. For some reason the sight of Charles seemed to be making him unwell. It was as though he were looking at Charles, but seeing someone else. Eventually Jarvis found a cab to take the Manettes home. As soon as they had gone, a man stepped out of the darkness. It was Sydney.

Up to now, no one had even acknowledged Sydney's part in the acquittal – Mr. Stryver had been far too busy taking the credit. Jarvis felt he did not like the fellow, even though he had saved Charles' life. A brief, tense conversation followed before Jarvis made his excuses and returned to the bank. Sydney and Charles were left alone outside the Old Bailey, two almost-strangers united by an uncanny similarity of looks.

Sydney, who'd been drinking steadily, offered to show Charles the nearest tavern for dinner. He continued to drink as Charles ate, staring at him fixedly. Eventually he spoke.

"Now your wine's here, Mr. Darnay, why don't you make a toast?"

"What toast?"

"The one that's on your mind."

"Well, to Miss Manette then!"

"Miss Manette," the drunk repeated. Then, looking his companion full in the face, Sydney flung his glass against the wall, where it shattered into pieces.

"How does it feel to have such a woman crying for you, Mr. Darnay?"

Charles remained silent, unsure how to answer.

Sydney spoke again, "Do you think I particularly like you?"

"No, I don't think you do," replied Charles.

"I don't think I do either," mused Sydney.

"Nonetheless, I'm aware I owe my life to you, so let me pay the bill anyway."

"Are you paying for everything?" asked Sydney.

"Yes."

"In that case, I'll have another bottle of wine."

As Charles left, Sydney called out, "You despise me because I've been drinking, but I'll tell you why I drink. I'm a disappointed man in a drudge of a job. I care for no man on earth and no man cares for me."

After Charles had gone, Sydney stared into the mirror. "Why should you like a man just because he looks like you?" he asked himself. "If only I could have changed places with him in court, those blue eyes would have been looking at me. But I couldn't change places with him. How I hate the man!"

Sydney finished his bottle of wine, told the servant to wake him at ten o'clock and slumped down against the table, with his head on his hands and the candle dripping hot wax onto the top of his head.

In those days, many men drank hard. Stryver and Sydney were no exception. They also worked as hard as they drank. Stryver was much in demand at the Old Bailey, and he never worked on a case without Sydney's help. Stryver was seen as a lion of the legal world. Eventually it got around that, while Sydney would never be a lion, he was an amazingly good jackal – quieter, less regal, but just as deadly a hunter.

At ten o'clock that night, Sydney made his way to Stryver's chambers. For several hours they worked together in a dingy room, the floor covered with papers, the walls covered with books. They talked about the day's case and Stryver congratulated his jackal on his essential part in it. Yet Sydney was obviously in a rough temper.

"The old Sydney Carton of our school days – up one minute, down the next. What's the matter with you tonight?" asked Stryver.

"Ah yes, our school days! Even then I did exercises for other boys and seldom did my own."

"I've often wondered why."

"God knows, that's just my way I suppose."

"Well, your way is a lame one. Now, as then, you have no energy or purpose. Why don't you make more effort? You could make a success of yourself. Look at me! We started together, but while I've gone

44

steaming ahead, you seem determined to hold yourself back."

"You've fallen into your rank and I into mine," replied Sydney. "Even when we were students in Paris, you were going places while I was always in trouble!"

"Why are you so gloomy, when we should be celebrating? Think of something pleasant... how about the pretty witness?"

"Which pretty witness?" asked Sydney carelessly, perhaps too carelessly.

"The doctor's daughter, of course!"

"You think she's pretty?"

"Don't you?"

"No. She's just a golden-haired doll, nothing remarkable."

"Have you got eyes, man? You must have been the only man in the courtroom not to find her remarkable. Though of course you were the first to notice when she fainted."

"A blind man could see a woman faint when she's sat that close to him! Anyway I'm tired and drunk and sick of today's trial. It's over, and I'm going to bed." With that, Sydney left the room and walked upstairs. Once out of Stryver's sight, his whole bearing changed. Alone in his room, this arrogant, careless man threw himself down on the bed and cried silently all night long.

Hundreds of People

The Manettes lived in a quiet London street near Soho Square. One sunny Sunday afternoon, four months after the trial, Jarvis was on his way to their house for dinner. At that time, London was not as built up as it is today. There were fewer houses and more trees – the Manettes' house was shaded by a big plane tree with rustling, green leaves.

When Jarvis arrived, the only person at home was Miss Pross, who was cooking. So Jarvis wandered through the house waiting for the Manettes. It was such a warm day, all the doors had been left open to let air circulate. So for the first time Jarvis saw into Dr. Manette's room. He was shocked to see the shoemaker's workbench and tools beside the bed.

While Jarvis was gazing at this unexpected sight, Miss Pross appeared, obviously in a mood about something. Jarvis discovered she was fretting about the "hundreds of people" who kept coming to the house to visit Lucie. He asked if there were really so many as "hundreds", to which she obstinately replied that there were – though Jarvis suspected the one person she was really jealous of was Charles Darnay, who'd become a regular visitor.

It was then that Miss Pross began talking about her brother, Solomon, and what he might have achieved – "if he hadn't made just one mistake in life". Jarvis knew that her brother's "one mistake" had been to gamble away all the money his sister possessed, and then to abandon her to live in poverty when his schemes failed. Yet she missed him still, and forgave him the horrible things he'd done to her, simply because he was her brother.

After listening politely for a while, Jarvis raised the question he had been longing to ask.

"Does the doctor ever talk about his shoemaking time?"

"Never."

"Yet he keeps his tools and bench beside his bed…"

"I didn't say he doesn't think of it, just that he never talks about it. I believe he thinks about it a great deal of the time."

"Do you think Dr. Manette can remember the name of the person who imprisoned him?"

"To be honest," she replied, "I think he's afraid of the subject. He never mentions it, but often I hear him at night, pacing up and down his room as if he's back in his cell. If Lucie gets up and goes to him, he doesn't say a word. They just walk together till the moment's passed. Then he goes back to sleep."

At that moment they heard Lucie and her father walking up the path. When Dr. Manette came in, he was in such good spirits that Jarvis stopped worrying about the shoemaking equipment and settled down to a good meal. The evening was so warm that, after dinner, they went outside to sit under the plane tree. Here they were joined, much to Miss Pross's annoyance, by Charles. He told them of a story he'd heard when he'd been held prisoner in the Tower of London before his trial.

"Some workmen found an old dungeon which had been bricked up and forgotten. Every stone seemed to be covered by inscriptions carved by prisoners: dates, names, prayers, complaints. On one cornerstone someone had carved three letters, D, I, C – or perhaps G. There was no record of a prisoner with those initials, and nobody could guess who it could have been, until someone suggested they weren't initials at all, but an instruction to dig.

"So they did, and they found the remains of a little bag containing paper the prisoner had written on – all turned to dust. What the unknown prisoner had written will never be read, but he had written something, and hidden it away from the jailer."

"Father!" Lucie suddenly called out. For as the story was finishing, the doctor had stood up and clutched his head as though in pain. "You're ill!"

Her voice seemed to bring him back from another world.

"No," he said, "not ill. It's... it's started to rain and it made me start. Come on, let's escape inside."

Then he refused to discuss the subject any further. They all hurried into the house, where they were soon joined by Sydney Carton. Jarvis noticed with amusement that Miss Pross looked more agitated still. He guessed that Charles and Sydney made up the sum total of Miss Pross's "hundreds of people".

The rain turned into a huge storm, with crashing thunder and a heavy, insistent downpour. The noise was so loud it became impossible for the little party to hear each other speak, so they sat in silence watching lightning rip across the sky. It was one o'clock in the morning before the weather had cleared enough to allow Jarvis to walk home, accompanied by Jerry as protection against muggers and highwaymen.

"What a night, Jerry! On a night like this I almost expect to see the dead come out of their graves."

"I don't expect I shall ever see such a night as would do that, sir," replied Jerry, dourly.

The Aristocrat

Monseigneur, one of the most important lords in the French court, held his fortnightly reception at a hotel in Paris. People flocked to him hoping for help with their problems. This great lord lived in the kind of opulent luxury common to all wealthy French men and women of the time, but which people today can hardly imagine. When he wanted to drink hot chocolate, it took not only a cook to make it, but four men to serve it. One to carry the pot into the room, one to froth the chocolate, one to hand Monseigneur a napkin and finally, one man to pour out the chocolate. It seemed almost incredible that Monseigneur deigned to do anything so mundane as actually drink it himself!

He was disliked by many of his own class as well as by the poor – though the aristocrats disliked him because they longed to have his power. He moved in the highest social circles, a life of glittering parties, operas and plays. While the poor died of starvation on the streets every day, Monseigneur ate heartily and frequently, and still required five people to bring him one simple pot of hot chocolate.

Most of those who attended his fortnightly receptions were disappointed. Today was no exception. Before he'd seen even half the people there, he became bored and broke off to dress for his evening appointment. The waiting crowd gradually dispersed. Last to leave was a haughty-faced man of about sixty, who cursed the absent lord to the devil as he walked to his carriage. He'd particularly wanted Monseigneur to help him deal with a pressing family problem. This man was handsomely dressed and obviously an aristocrat – you could tell by the crest on his carriage door. His face, though cruel when it was animated, normally looked like an emotionless mask through which his frighteningly piercing eyes bored two narrow holes.

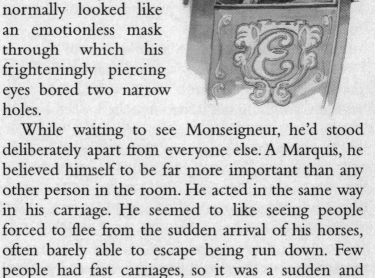

While waiting to see Monseigneur, he'd stood deliberately apart from everyone else. A Marquis, he believed himself to be far more important than any other person in the room. He acted in the same way in his carriage. He seemed to like seeing people forced to flee from the sudden arrival of his horses, often barely able to escape being run down. Few people had fast carriages, so it was a sudden and terrifying shock to find one thundering along a street at a breakneck pace.

With a wild rattle and clatter, the Marquis's carriage dashed through the streets. Men and women screamed in front of it and snatched children out of the way. Suddenly, swooping around a corner by a fountain, the wheels gave a sickening jolt, and a loud cry was heard as the horses reared and stopped.

"What's happening?" asked the nobleman, calmly looking out of his window.

"Pardon, my lord Marquis, but it is a child," replied a servant.

"Why is that man making such an appalling noise? Is it his child?"

"Yes, sir."

A tall man who'd been stooped over the fountain holding the child's body suddenly reared up and rushed at the carriage.

"Killed!" he shrieked. "My child is dead!"

All eyes turned to the Marquis, but submissively, as people knew his servants were armed. His eyes registered nothing but irritation as he looked back at them.

"It's extraordinary to me that you people can't take more care of your children. One or other of them is forever in the way of my carriage. I hope you haven't damaged my valuable horses! Here, take that."

He threw a gold coin to the dead child's father, with the air of a gentleman who'd accidentally broken some common thing but could easily afford to pay for it. As he did so, another man arrived. The dead child's father grabbed him and sobbed bitterly on his shoulder.

"Be brave, my friend," spoke the newcomer. "It's better he died quickly than lived in a world of pain. He's happy now – could he have lived nearly so happily upon this earth?"

The Marquis smiled and spoke to the newcomer, "A philosopher! What's your name?"

"Defarge."

"Here, take this, philosopher Defarge," said the Marquis, throwing another gold coin out of the window.

The carriage leaped forward and drove away. Suddenly a gold coin came flying through the carriage window, narrowly missing the Marquis's head. Furious, he shouted to his servants to stop.

"Who threw that?" he demanded.

Defarge had gone and the distraught father just lay weeping on the ground. Beside him stood a stout woman, knitting and staring at the Marquis. Cursing them all, he shouted to his servants to get moving again.

His carriage continued on its way, the people went back to their drudgery, the fountain continued to flow and the woman kept on knitting. All things ran their course.

The carriage drove on through a beautiful landscape, but the crops which should have been growing there were few and far between. The people who tended the land and depended upon its crops were equally thin and sparse. Yet the Marquis didn't notice or care. By rights he was responsible for the village and its people, but all he wanted was their rent money. Otherwise he barely considered them.

He did, however, notice one man: a road mender in a blue cap. The Marquis realized he had seen him twice already. Finding this suspicious, he shouted for the man to be brought to him.

"You! How come we've passed you twice? Why are you so interested in staring at my carriage?"

"I beg your pardon, sir, I wasn't staring at you but at the man underneath."

"What man? What do you mean?"

"He was hanging underneath the carriage my lord, like a ghost swaying in the wind."

"What was he like?"

"A tall man, white all over from the road dust. Tall and white as a ghost!"

The servants examined the carriage, but found no one.

"Pah! You stupid man!" exclaimed the Marquis. "Seeing a thief on my carriage and not telling me until he's gone. If anyone sees the thief again, I want you to seize him."

The sun was beginning to set behind the hills. As the carriage reached the peak of the steepest hill, a little burial ground could be seen. There were thin humps in the ground, but barely any were marked with the names of the deceased. Kneeling at the side of the cemetery was a young woman. As she heard the carriage, she got up and approached the window.

"Please my lord, a petition!"

"What now? Why do you people always have petitions?"

"Please sir, my husband..."

"What? Can't he pay his debts?"

"He has no more debts to pay. He's dead, he died from hunger."

"So, what can I do about it?"

"Please, please sir, could you allow me a little cross, a little piece of stone to mark his grave? Or by the time I die, no one will know where he is to bury me with him..." But her last words were spoken to deaf ears. The valet had already pushed her away and the horses trotted briskly on, ignoring her cries.

The sky was dark as the Marquis reached his home, a large, high-roofed chateau surrounded by enormous trees. It was lit with expensive torches.

"Has Monsieur Charles arrived from England?" he inquired as he entered the house.

"Not yet, my lord."

The Marquis's chateau was a heavy mass of stone. In front of it lay a large, stone courtyard from which two stone staircases swept up to an imposing terrace and a huge door. Everything about it was stony: the balustrades, the heavy urns, the decorations on the facade. There were stone flowers, stone heads of lions and stone faces. It was as if a mythical Gorgon had looked at the building and turned everything to cold, unyielding rock.

The Marquis strode up the steps and into the great hall. Its walls were grim with old boar-hunting spears, swords, knives and heavy riding whips – some of which had been used fatally to discipline tenants who couldn't pay their dues. He reached his private apartment, where a supper table was laid for two.

"I can't wait any longer for my nephew," he instructed his servants. "I'll be ready to eat in quarter of an hour, whether he's here or not."

As he sat eating alone, waited on by several men, the Marquis heard a noise.

"What's that? Open the blinds."

But nothing could be seen outside.

Halfway through his supper, the sound of wheels was heard. Within minutes his nephew was being shown into the room. In England, he went by the name of Charles Darnay.

The Marquis received Charles with formal politeness, but they did not shake hands.

"You've been a long time in coming."

"On the contrary, I came direct from London," answered Charles.

"I didn't mean a long time on the journey, I meant it's taken you a long time to get around to making it."

"I've been detained by... business."

That was the extent of their conversation as long as servants were present. They finished their meal in silence. When they were alone over coffee, Charles began to speak.

"I've come back, as I'm sure you're aware, still pursuing the object that took me away."

"I know."

"No doubt you also know it's been at times a perilous journey – made, I should imagine, more dangerous by your own intervention against me."

"Surely not," smiled the uncle.

"I know you would stop me by any means. In fact, I think it's more due to your bad luck than my good luck that I haven't yet been imprisoned in France."

Again, the Marquis merely smiled.

"I presume," continued Charles, "your reception in Paris was as usual a cold one – luckily for me."

The Marquis stopped smiling and replied, "I'm not so sure it was lucky. A spell in prison might be exactly the thing to make you realize your true position. How can you attack the life our family's enjoyed for centuries? Do you have no idea how ridiculous your actions make our family name, the noble name of

Evrémonde? There have already been enough changes, ridding us of privilege after privilege, without my own flesh and blood attempting to change the natural order of things."

"As you say, we've behaved according to our 'privileges' for centuries now. So much so that I believe our name to be more detested than any other in France," admitted Charles gloomily.

"Let's hope so — to be detested means we have power and rank!"

"There is no one around here who will ever look at me with anything except hatred and fear."

"A compliment!" exclaimed the Marquis. "Repression of the peasants is the only sensible solution for families like ours. I will preserve the nobility of our family, even if you, my only living relative, will not."

"But we have done wrong, and we're still reaping the fruits of that wrong."

"*We've* done wrong? As far as I can remember, *you've* given me no assistance in any matter at all."

"Maybe not myself, but my father was your twin. How can I separate myself from the evil that he did? Especially when my mother begged me to make right the wrongs he committed."

"Your pleas are lost on me. I intend to die preserving the system under which I've lived — and you, with your ridiculous radical ideas, are powerless to stop me. One day, of course, all this shall be yours." He laughed as he indicated the heavily mortgaged home. "But I intend to live a very, very long time, happy to keep you from your inheritance!"

"I would renounce this even if you died tomorrow. If this property were ever to come to me, I'd gladly hand it over to the people who work the land, for they're the ones who rightfully own it. There's a curse on this place as long as our family lives here."

"And in England, don't they mind having a member of such an 'evil' family living among them?"

"I no longer bear our name, nor have any wish to do so. In England, I'm known by a new name, one I chose for myself."

"I hear England is quite a refuge for our dispossessed compatriots. Tell me, do you know of a French doctor living there, with a daughter?"

"Yes."

"Yes – how ironic," mumbled the Marquis, as he turned to leave the room. "Good night."

The following morning, a whispering could be heard in the village. It seemed a new stone face had been discovered at the chateau. It lay on the pillow of the Marquis. He was lying on his bed, a knife driven through his stony heart. Attached to the knife was a frill of paper, on which was scrawled: *"Drive him fast to his tomb. From JACQUES."*

Love and Marriage

A year had passed and Charles Darnay was well-established in England as a French teacher and translator. He worked hard, earning a modest but decent wage, and acquiring a good reputation. He spent half his time in Cambridge, teaching university students, and the other half in London. He was doing his best to forget the chateau, and his real name and everything associated with it. But it was impossible to forget. And he spent every day thinking about Lucie Manette.

Charles had fallen in love with Lucie during his trial, but had not yet told her. Instead, he contented himself with being her friend. One day, when he knew Lucie and Miss Pross would be out, he called on Dr. Manette.

"Charles, we've missed you for the last few days," said the doctor. "Sydney and Mr. Stryver have both been here..." (at this Charles winced) "... and we wondered when you'd next be in London."

"Dr. Manette, I need to speak to you about Lucie."

The doctor smiled and asked, "Are you in love with her?"

"Yes, I love her more than I had believed possible."

"Have you spoken to her about it?"

"No. I needed to speak to you first. Like you I'm

a voluntary exile from France, driven away from it, as you were, by its oppressions and miseries. But, unlike you, I bear a name that could make me hated in spite of my own actions. I don't want to have any secrets from you; the name you know me by is assumed. I want to tell you the truth about myself..."

"Stop!" shouted the doctor. "Don't tell me yet. I don't need... I don't want to know. If Lucie agrees to marry you, you can tell me on the morning of the wedding. Please don't tell me before. Do you promise?"

"Willingly."

"Good. You should go home. She'll be back soon and you don't want her to know we've been talking about her."

Charles left, feeling happier than he'd felt for a year. The doctor, on the other hand, felt worse.

When Lucie returned home, she was surprised to find the sitting room empty. She called for her father and, when he didn't answer, she searched the house. As she neared his bedroom, she could hear a low hammering sound, which chilled her blood. Steeling herself, she entered the room and spoke to him gently, asking him to leave his shoemaking for the night. Then they walked up and down, up and down, in silence, until he was tired enough to sleep. The next morning, the workbench and tools were back to normal, and no mention was made of it again.

On that same night, Mr. Stryver and Sydney were hard at work in Stryver's Chambers.

"Sydney, I've something to say that may come as a shock," said Stryver, looking up from his papers. "I know this is totally against my nature, but I've decided to get married."

"Really? Who to?"

"Guess."

"Do I know her?"

"Guess!"

"I'm not guessing anything at five in the morning, after a night of wine punch and solid work!"

"Sometimes I despair of you. You're such an insensitive dog."

"Whereas you, of course, have the soul of a romantic poet," retorted Sydney sarcastically.

"I don't claim to be romantic, but at least I know how to be agreeable to a woman. You've had the same advantages as I've had, but you seem to have no social skills at all. For instance, I've been ashamed of your moroseness at Dr. Manette's house. How could you act that way in front of Miss Manette?"

Sydney returned to the bowl of punch, drank a glass and laughed – though he'd actually never felt less like laughing.

"Stop talking about me and get back to your wedding plans. Who is she?"

"Well, I'm worried about telling you because

you once called her an unremarkable, 'golden-haired doll'. I am, of course, talking about Miss Manette."

Sydney seemed to flinch.

"Are you surprised?"

Sydney took another gulp of punch. "Why should I be?"

"D'you approve?"

"Why shouldn't I?" asked Sydney, finishing his glass and refilling it. "Have you asked her?"

"No, not yet. I know I've always said I'm not the marrying type, and it's not as if she has much money, but she's very pretty and I think it would be a bonus for her to marry a man with my advantages. In fact, I've changed my mind entirely about marriage – and I've been thinking about you too, Sydney. Your life's too dissolute. You should settle down. Find a respectable woman with a bit of property, who could take care of you, and marry her."

"I'll think about it," said Sydney, carrying the rest of the punch out of the room.

Mr. Stryver, having made up his mind to do Lucie the good turn of marrying her, decided to tell her of her good fortune right away. He was about to leave town for the summer, and wanted to get it over with before he left.

As he was walking towards Soho, he went past Tellson's and thought of passing on the good news to Jarvis. A peculiar thing about Mr. Stryver was that he always managed to look too big for any situation and, in the confined offices of the bank, he seemed positively enormous. Jarvis, though startled by this sudden visitor, greeted him in a business-like manner. But when Stryver confided the true reason for the visit, Jarvis looked very worried and exclaimed, "Oh no!" before he could stop himself. He couldn't imagine Lucie ever being happy with such a self-satisfied man.

Mr. Stryver was, understandably, put out by the banker's comment and asked what he meant.

"I just meant... I don't think it's a good idea... to do such a thing without some idea that you might succeed," Jarvis eventually admitted.

Mr. Stryver was even less pleased. "Why shouldn't I succeed? Is the lady some kind of simple fool?"

"No sir, and I will not hear anyone speaking disrespectfully of Miss Manette!" Then, he added more calmly, "I just meant I've never heard either of you talk about love, and I'm not sure she feels the way you do. May I suggest I talk to her subtly on your behalf and find out how she feels about it?"

Mr. Stryver reluctantly agreed, his confidence having taken something of a bashing.

"I've been asked to dinner with the Manettes tonight," continued Jarvis. "I could come to your lodgings afterwards if you like?"

"Alright," said Mr. Stryver. "Thank you." (Though he didn't mean it.) Then he turned abruptly and left. All the way home, Jarvis's comments rankled, and Stryver became determined he wouldn't let any woman get the better of him.

So, when a nervous Jarvis arrived at Stryver's

Chambers later that night and started apologetically to explain he didn't think Mr. Stryver should propose to Lucie, the lawyer pretended almost to have forgotten their earlier conversation.

"Thank you, Mr. Lorry, I'm much obliged. To be honest it's probably a much better idea not to do so, as you say. After all, a man in my position really can't gain much by marrying. I just thought it would be a good opportunity for the girl, but never mind." With that, he ushered an astonished Jarvis to the door.

When the banker had gone, Mr. Stryver lay back on his sofa and blinked repeatedly at the ceiling, as though he had something in his eyes.

If Sydney Carton shone anywhere, it was definitely not at the Manettes' house. If he could be persuaded to talk, his conversation was always interesting. But, as he didn't have the confidence to talk very often, his silence was often misinterpreted as rudeness. His aloof manner, however, concealed a sensitive soul. He was having trouble sleeping and, at night, could frequently be seen pacing the streets around the Manettes' home.

One day, Mr. Stryver told Sydney that he had thought better of "that marrying matter", and left for a summer holiday in Devon. Deprived of his usual distraction of work, Sydney found himself walking to Soho, where he discovered Lucie on her own. She was embarrassed at first, as he often made her feel uncomfortable, but as she looked at his face she grew concerned.

"Are you ill?" she asked.

"No, but the life I lead isn't very healthy."

"Then why do you live it? Why not change?"

There were tears in his voice as he answered, "It's too late for that. Forgive me, I don't mean to make you uncomfortable, but I must talk to you."

Then Sydney told her. He told her he was in love with her, although he knew she didn't love him and never would. But he wanted her to know the reason he was always so sullen in her company was because he didn't know any other way to act. Unlike Mr. Stryver, who had convinced himself he would be doing Lucie a good turn, Sydney expected absolutely nothing in return; he just wanted her to know how he felt. All he asked was that she tell no one of this conversation.

"You needn't worry," he concluded, "that I will ever embarrass you by mentioning this again. I just had to tell you, so that at the end of my life I can be happy I was able to talk to you. For you and anyone you love, I would do anything, I want you to know that. All I ask is that occasionally you think of me kindly, and know always that there's one man who would willingly give his life for you."

Then he said goodbye and left her.

The Honest Tradesman

Jerry was sitting, bored, outside Tellson's Bank when he heard a commotion in the distance. It seemed to be getting nearer. He squinted his eyes to see where it was coming from and then called to his son, "Look! It's a funeral." The funeral procession consisted of nothing more than the coffin, the undertakers and one mourner, but it was accompanied by a large, jeering crowd hissing and yelling, "Spies!"

Funerals always held a fascination for Jerry, so he left his son to guard his post and ran to join the crowd.

"What's this about?" he asked.

"Spies!" was the general reply, until one man told him it was the funeral of "Roger Cly, an Old Bailey spy".

Jerry remembered the trial he'd seen at the Old Bailey. "I've seen him! So he's dead then is he?"

"Can't be too dead as far as we're concerned," answered the man.

The crowd murmured general agreement. Then some of the mob suggested separating the coffin and its mourner from the hearse. The horses' way was barred and hands started to tug at the coach doors.

The solitary mourner, quick on his feet, managed to escape, leaving behind several articles of clothing pulled from him as he fled. The nearby traders rapidly shut up their shops – a crowd in those times stopped at nothing.

When the coffin proved too difficult to pull out of the hearse, someone suggested they accompany it to the graveyard instead. New "mourners" joined all along the route, including an unfortunate dancing bear and his owner, a common sight in London in those days. This gave the funeral procession something of the air of a carnival.

Jerry kept well away from the crowd. The undertakers' destination was the old church of Saint Pancras, where he watched the coffin finally being put into the ground. By this time, the mob was out of control, breaking windows, looting pubs and shops, and assaulting passersby. Meanwhile, Jerry remained chatting to the undertakers.

On his way back to Tellson's, he stopped at the house of a distinguished surgeon – somewhat surprisingly as it was unlikely Jerry could have afforded the surgeon's fees. He remained there, however, for a little while before heading back to work.

That evening, Jerry remonstrated with his wife once again about her praying.

"If anything goes wrong for me tonight, woman, I shall know you've been praying against me again, and I'll make you pay for it," he threatened.

"You're going out tonight?" she inquired timidly.

"Yes, I'm going fishing."

"Can I come too?" asked young Jerry.

"No, you can't. And you," he added to his wife, "remember no praying and no complaining. If I bring home a joint of meat or fish for breakfast, don't you dare refuse it like before."

Then he ate his meal in silence, glowering at his wife from time to time.

Later that night, when young Jerry and Mrs. Cruncher were in bed, Jerry opened a locked cupboard and took out a sack, a crowbar, a rope and a chain – all of which he seemed to think essential for fishing. Then he left the house. A few seconds later, young Jerry slipped out after him. His father was joined by two other men. They walked for a long time before finally reaching a high wall, which they scaled nimbly. Frightened of doing the same, in case he made a noise, young Jerry crept along to the gate, through which he spied his father and companions creeping through a graveyard.

What followed bore no resemblance to fishing. Instead, they began digging up what looked like a new grave. Young Jerry watched, scared but transfixed, as bit by bit the coffin was brought to the surface. He watched as his father began to lever off the lid. Then, too terrified of seeing what was inside, young Jerry jumped up and ran home as fast as he could. All the way he imagined the coffin's terrible inhabitant chasing him through the darkness. It hid in doorways and jumped out at him from the

shadows, it lay in wait to trip him as he ran, it almost caught him several times, but at last he got home, terrified out of his wits. He ran up the stairs and threw himself into bed, where he fell at once into an exhausted sleep.

The next morning, he awoke to a violent fight and the sound of his father beating his mother's head against the wall.

"Why do you oppose me at every turn?" he was shouting.

"I try to be a good wife, Jerry," she was crying.

"Is it the job of a good wife to oppose her

70

husband's business?"

"You hadn't taken to the dreadful business when we got married."

"A true wife would support her husband no matter what his business. And I won't have you praying to thwart me." He beat her a couple more times for good measure, then shouted at her to get his breakfast.

There was no meat or fish, or indeed much at all for breakfast. Jerry was in a furious mood and the table was silent. At the usual time he set off for Tellson's, carrying his stool, with his son beside him.

"Father," asked young Jerry, making sure the stool was between him and his parent. "What's a resurrection man?"

Jerry stopped walking before saying, "How should I know?"

"I thought you knew everything, father."

"Hmm, well, he's a tradesman, a worker who provides special services for scientists and surgeons."

"He supplies dead bodies doesn't he?"

"I believe so."

"Father, I should like to be a resurrection man when I grow up."

Mr. Cruncher smiled. "That boy may yet make up for the shortcomings of his mother," he said to himself, as he took up his post outside the bank.

Knitting

The drinking had begun earlier than usual in Defarge's wine shop, yet an air of gloom hung over it nevertheless. Defarge was not at home. His wife sat behind the counter, knitting and serving customers. At noon Defarge appeared with a road mender, who was wearing a blue cap.

"Good day," said Defarge to his customers. "It's bad weather," he added, at which point a man got up and went out.

Then Defarge turned to his wife. "I've come several miles with this man, Jacques. I met him by chance and asked him to have a drink with us."

While Madame Defarge was pouring the wine, two other men silently left the shop. Then Defarge offered to show Jacques the apartment he'd told him about, and they left together.

Crossing the courtyard, they climbed to the room where Dr. Manette had once stayed. The three men who'd left the wine shop were waiting for them.

Defarge closed the door and spoke in a subdued voice, "Jacques One, Jacques Two, Jacques Three, this is the witness I told you of. Speak, Jacques Five."

The road mender then told his story. He described the tall man covered in white dust he'd seen hanging beneath the Marquis's carriage the year before. He spoke of the Marquis's wrath and what he had told him. At first, the others were angry that Jacques Five had given such an accurate description of Gaspard. But, as Defarge pointed out, Jacques Five had never before heard of their group, or of the death of the child beneath the carriage's wheels.

"The guards sought the man for nearly a year without finding him," continued the road mender.

"But, unhappily, they did find him," added Defarge.

The road mender then described how the soldiers had led Gaspard, bound and gagged, beating him with their guns as they went. "They led him through the village to the prison. The whole village was buzzing with talk. They said he wouldn't be killed because a petition had been made to the king. I don't know if that was true."

"It is true," said Jacques One. "Defarge himself took a petition to the king and queen in their carriage. They tried to run him down, but he avoided them, the petition still in his hand. Then the king's guards surrounded him and beat him."

The road mender continued, describing how the prisoner was eventually taken into the village, where he was publicly tortured, then hanged above the fountain. He told them the dead man's body was still hanging there, poisoning the fountain and leaving the people without drinking water, but no one dared move it for fear the soldiers would kill them too.

"The whole village is dying," he said, "so I left to meet with this man, as I'd been instructed to do, to tell you my story."

Defarge asked the road mender to wait outside the door. When he'd gone, Jacques One asked, "What do you think? To be registered?"

"To be registered as doomed to destruction," answered Defarge.

"The chateau and the whole family," added another Jacques, and all agreed.

"Are you sure our register is safe from prying eyes?" asked Jacques Two.

"Quite sure," answered Defarge. "It's kept in my wife's knitting, in her own secret code of stitches and symbols. No one else would ever be able to decipher it – likewise no man whose name is on that register could ever erase it."

"What will we do with the road mender?"

"I'll take care of him. He wants to stay a day or two to see the king and queen, then he'll go home," said Defarge.

The others looked at him in amazement. "He wants to see the king and queen and you've allowed him into our group. Isn't that dangerous?"

"He knows nothing, at least nothing that is of any more danger to ourselves than to him. Even if he wanted to tell, it would only lead him straight to the gallows. He's safe, he's just a simple countryman."

"But he wants to see the king and queen!"

"Jacques," replied Defarge, "if you want a dog to bring down his prey, you must first show it to him."

On Sunday, the road mender set out for Versailles with the Defarges. He was nervous of Madame Defarge, who knitted all the way.

"You work hard, madame," commented a man nearby.

"Yes, I have a lot to do."

"What do you make?"

"Many things... shrouds, for instance," she answered.

When the king and queen appeared in their carriage, the crowd shouted and cheered. The road mender, who'd never before seen such a sight, cheered and clapped loudest of all.

Afterwards, Madame Defarge asked him, "You thought that was a fine spectacle, the king and queen with their expensive clothes and their beautiful carriage?"

"Yes, madame."

"Would you fight to have a share in such riches?"

"Truly, yes."

"Well, the time may come for fighting. Now, go home."

The Defarges returned to Saint Antoine and the road mender made his way home. As usual, when the public coach arrived at the city gate, it was stopped by the guards. Monsieur Defarge knew the guards and one of the policemen, so he got out of the coach to talk to them.

Later, Madame Defarge asked, "What did Jacques of the police tell you?"

"That there's another spy commissioned for Saint Antoine. He's English, named John Barsad. He's about forty, five feet nine inches tall, with black hair, dark eyes and a dark complexion. Oh yes, and his nose bends slightly to the left."

Madame Defarge laughed, "What a perfect description! He'll be registered tomorrow."

Back in the wine shop, Madame Defarge counted the day's takings, while her husband paced up and down, smoking his pipe. Tonight he appeared agitated, and commented how stale and sour the shop smelled.

"It's no different from usual," his wife insisted calmly. "You're just tired."

"I am."

"And a little depressed," she added. Then she exclaimed, with feeling, "Oh, you men!"

"But my dear..." began Defarge.

"Admit it, you're scared."

"Well... it just seems to drag on such a long time."

"Of course it takes time! When has vengeance ever been achieved quickly? It may seem a long time, but believe me it keeps on advancing. Look around you every day, consider the awful stories constantly told to the Jacquerie. Our cause will never die."

"But maybe we'll never see the triumph," he said despondently.

"Maybe not, but we'll have helped. Anyway, I think the time could be nearer than you know. And while you men worry and complain, we women will stop at nothing!"

"I will also stop at nothing," he cried, reddening as though charged with cowardice.

"I know, my dear," she said, as though talking to a child. "I know."

The next day Madame Defarge was sitting behind the counter, knitting. A rose lay beside her. When a stranger entered the shop, she laid down the knitting, picked up the rose and pinned it onto her hat. Then she greeted the man. It was a curious thing, but as soon as Madame Defarge pinned the rose to her hat, the customers slowly began to leave.

"Good day, madame," said the stranger.

She continued knitting. He matched Defarge's description of the new spy exactly. He asked for a cognac and a glass of water, which she fetched for him, then he made small talk.

"You knit very well. It's a pretty pattern too."

"You think so?" she asked, with what looked like a smile of genuine amusement.

The sight of a rose on Madame Defarge's hat seemed to have a curious effect on the inhabitants of Saint Antoine. Several men peered in through the shop window, but all left without entering. The spy was puzzled. He tried to spot some kind of signal passing between the woman behind the counter and the men at the door, but there was nothing.

"J-O-H-N," thought Madame Defarge, as she knitted. "Stay a little longer and I'll finish knitting B-A-R-S-A-D before you go."

"Business seems bad," he ventured.

"It is; the people are too poor."

"Ah yes, the unfortunate, oppressed people, as you say."

"As *you* say," she corrected him.

"But naturally you think so too?"

"We have enough to do to keep this shop going without having time to think!"

"It's a bad business, this Gaspard's execution," sighed the spy.

"He knew the price he'd pay for his actions," she commented, coolly. "Ah, here's my husband."

As Defarge entered, the newcomer greeted him confidently, "Good day, Jacques."

Defarge seemed surprised. "I'm sorry sir, but my name is Ernest."

The spy looked uncomfortable. "I'm sorry... um, as I was saying just now to your wife, I was sad to hear about poor Gaspard. I am sure feelings must be running high in Saint Antoine."

"No one's said anything to me," answered Defarge.

The spy tried again. "I hear you're acquainted with Dr. Manette?"

"Yes, I am."

"I suppose you hear regularly from him and his daughter in England?"

"No," answered Madame Defarge. "A couple of letters at first, but since then nothing."

"So you don't know she's getting married?"

"Getting married?" snorted the woman, "She was pretty enough to be married years ago. You English are so cold!"

"Oh, you know I'm English?" he asked, taken aback.

"I can tell by your accent."

"Oh. Well yes, Miss Manette's going to be married. To a Frenchman in fact. Isn't it curious that she's marrying the nephew of that Marquis killed by poor Gaspard? Of course, in England he's not known by his family name; he calls himself Charles Darnay."

Madame Defarge didn't drop a single stitch, but her husband's hand shook as he filled his pipe. The spy took note – it was his job to observe such details – but that was all he took away with him when he left the shop that afternoon.

"Do you think it's true?" Defarge asked his wife immediately the spy had gone.

"Maybe."

"But if it is..."

"If it is... ?" she repeated, menacingly.

He faltered, "If it is, I hope for her sake that fate keeps her husband out of France."

"He will go wherever fate takes him," said Madame Defarge, rolling up her knitting. Then she unpinned the rose from her hat and the shop filled up again.

That night, a group of women knitted together in Saint Antoine. Madame Defarge exchanged brief conversations with each. Her husband stood in the doorway watching her. "A strong woman, an admirable woman," he told himself, inhaling deeply from his pipe.

Family Matters

One memorable summer evening, the sun was setting magnificently in the Soho sky while Dr. Manette and his daughter sat happily in their garden. Lucie was getting married the following morning.

"I'm so happy tonight," she told her father.

"I know," he replied. "And nothing could make me happier than seeing you in love. In prison I was always worried about you, so it's wonderful for me to see you like this."

This was the only time since the trial that Lucie had heard her father speak of his time in prison.

He continued, "So many nights I'd try to imagine the child I knew would have been born just a few months after I was captured. I tried to guess whether it would be a son who'd grow up to avenge me; there were times when I was desperate for vengeance. Other times I hoped fervently it would be a daughter, who'd simply grow up to be happy."

At this point, Miss Pross called them in to dinner. There were just the three of them at the table that evening, as Jarvis had tactfully stayed away and convention forbade a bride and groom from seeing each other the night before the wedding. But after the marriage, Charles would move into the Soho house, so Dr. Manette wouldn't be left alone.

That night, Lucie couldn't sleep. She was worried that her father talking about prison might have been a sign that his mind was unsettled, so she crept along the corridor to his room. Looking in, she could see he was fast asleep and the shoemaker's bench and tools were all in their usual places. She returned to her room, relieved.

The day of the wedding was sunny. Jarvis, who was the best man, and Miss Pross, the bridesmaid, were the only guests. Lucie was in her wedding dress and ready to leave for the church, but the three of them were standing waiting for the doctor and Charles, who'd been talking in the doctor's study for quite some time now. Eventually the door opened, and the doctor and Charles came out. The doctor looked dreadfully pale, though he dismissed it as nothing but wedding-day nerves. He took his daughter's arm and walked with her to the church.

After the wedding breakfast, Charles and Lucie Darnay left for their honeymoon. Almost at once, Jarvis observed a great change come over the doctor. He seemed to have regained the scared, lost look he had worn when they'd found him making shoes in Paris. Jarvis was reluctant to leave him, but had promised the bank he'd call in to check if there was any business he needed to deal with personally, so he left for a couple of hours.

When he returned to Soho, he was greeted by an ominous, low, knocking noise.

"Miss Pross," he called out, as he entered the house, "what's that?"

Miss Pross rushed into the hallway. She looked scared. "Mr. Lorry, I don't know what to do. He doesn't recognize me and he's making shoes!"

Jarvis ran to the doctor's room. "Alexandre, it's me, Jarvis."

The doctor looked at him blankly and went back to his work. He had removed his jacket, taken off his cravat and unbuttoned his shirt. To Jarvis, it even seemed as though his face had changed back to the way it had looked in Paris.

"I must finish this; it's a lady's walking shoe."

"But you are Dr. Manette. Look at me. This isn't your proper occupation, please put your tools down."

The doctor was adamant, however, and continued in his work. Jarvis gave up and left the room to talk to Miss Pross. They agreed to keep the doctor's relapse a secret. Miss Pross then wrote a letter to Lucie, explaining the doctor had been called away to an urgent case and would be unable to write to his daughter for a while.

For the first time in his life, Jarvis took time off work. He took up his post in the doctor's room, where he watched him carefully. When he needed a rest, Miss Pross would take over. Dr. Manette continued to work, stopping only to eat and drink whatever was given him. He still showed no signs of recognizing either of them. Jarvis spoke to him regularly, occasionally asking if he'd like to stop his work and come for a walk in the garden. Each time, the doctor looked astonished to be asked. He didn't ever accept the invitation, but each time the idea seemed to penetrate a little further. The idea that, if he wanted to, he could leave this room and walk around, that there were no jailers.

But after several days had passed, Jarvis became even more worried. By the ninth day it was obvious to both observers that the hands, which had by now made several pairs of shoes, were becoming frighteningly expert.

That night, Jarvis fell asleep in the little room next to the doctor's bedroom. He was woken by sunlight streaming through the window. He rubbed his eyes, got up and checked the doctor's room. Then he had to rub his eyes again. The shoemaker's bench and tools had been put aside, and the doctor sat reading, dressed in his usual morning clothes. Jarvis began to doubt whether the last nine days had really taken place at all.

It soon became apparent that Dr. Manette had no recollection of his illness – or of the past nine days – and thought Lucie's wedding had taken place the day before. When the newspaper revealed the real date, it made him agitated. So, when breakfast was over, Jarvis asked if he could talk to him, confidentially, as a medical man. He said he needed to consult him about a friend who'd been ill with mental shock. Dr. Manette understood at once.

"It's an old and prolonged shock," continued Jarvis, "from which he appeared to have recovered, but unfortunately there's been a slight relapse."

The doctor hesitated before asking, "How long did it last?"

"Nine days."

"Ah, I see," he nodded sadly. "You mentioned your friend has a daughter. Does she know?"

"No, only I and one other, a trusted servant and friend, know of it. Tell me doctor, how does this relapse come about? Is there danger of another? Can it be prevented?"

"I think it probable the relapse was anticipated. I think your friend dreaded it, but could do little to prevent it. It occurred because he was forcefully reminded of the original cause of the illness. However I think the relapse has passed and is unlikely to occur again, at least not as severely."

"There's one other thing," Jarvis said nervously. "When my friend was ill, he believed himself to have another occupation, shall I say, a blacksmith. All the time his forge was close by him. Don't you think it would be better if the forge was destroyed, so that such a relapse couldn't occur again?"

The doctor nodded in comprehension, but looked very upset. "It's hard to explain, but your friend would find it hard to part with his forge. You see, there was a time when it meant everything… it was his only relief from terror."

"Nonetheless," continued Jarvis carefully, "don't you think it would be healthier for the forge to be removed? For his daughter's sake, if not for his?"

There was a very long pause before the doctor

finally replied, "For his daughter, yes, you're right. But I'd ask one thing for your friend, and that is when you do destroy his forge, do it when he's nowhere near, so he doesn't see it happen."

Jarvis agreed.

Two weeks after the wedding, Dr. Manette joined Lucie and Charles in the country. That evening Jarvis and Miss Pross went into his bedroom armed with a hatchet, saw, chisel and hammer. Miss Pross held a candle to light the room as Jarvis hacked the shoemaker's bench to pieces. Anyone looking in and seeing their grim faces would have thought they were witnessing

a murder.

When the newlyweds returned home, the first person to appear and offer congratulations was Sydney Carton. As soon as he could, he took Charles to one side. He apologized for his comments after the trial and hoped Charles could forget what he'd said. Then he asked if they could be friends.

"Of course," said Charles politely, not really meaning it.

"No," said Sydney, "I don't just mean can we be polite to each other. I'd like us to be real friends."

Charles assented, telling Sydney the past was forgotten, though in truth his opinion of him was still low. It takes a long time to trust someone as a true friend, and Charles wasn't sure he would ever manage it in Sydney's case.

After Sydney had gone, Charles mentioned their conversation, somewhat dismissively, to Lucie, who reproached him.

"I think poor Sydney deserves more consideration and respect than you showed him tonight," she said.

"Really – why's that?" Charles asked, surprised. He knew from past conversations that Lucie felt uncomfortable around Sydney.

"I've changed my opinion of him recently and I think you should too. He may act brash and indifferent, but that's not what he's really like. Believe me, he has a good heart which he very seldom reveals, and there are deep wounds in it. I've seen it bleeding."

"I'm really sorry to have been so flippant then," said Charles, astounded. "I've always thought him just a careless, reckless fellow, but if you say he's good deep down, I'll believe you. I promise not to slight him again."

Lucie thanked him, adding gently, "Just remember how strong we are in our happiness, and how weak he is in his misery.

Echoing Footsteps

Lucie gave birth to a daughter, little Lucie, who grew up happily speaking both English and French, the languages of the two countries in her life. In their Soho house, Lucie often believed she could hear the softly echoing footsteps of people from the past. They mingled with the strong, safe footsteps of her husband, her father and Miss Pross, and the toddling steps of her child.

Their second baby was a boy, but he died in childhood. Children's deaths were much more common then than they are today, and all parents had to prepare themselves for the possibility that a baby might not live very long. But the shadow that came over Soho with his death lingered for a long time. Until now Lucie's family had seemed to live a charmed existence, but all that was soon to change.

Sydney came to visit about once every two months, when he'd sit and absorb their family life. He never, ever visited when drunk. As often happens in these cases, his love for Lucie gave him a special empathy with her children. He was the first stranger to whom little Lucie reached out her arms, and when her brother died, one of the last things he said was, "Kiss Sydney for me."

Mr. Stryver became even more successful in the

world of law and grew ever richer – although Sydney continued to do much of his work and grew no richer at all. Stryver married a large widow with property and three pudding-like sons. He offered these sons to Charles as pupils, but was so patronizing that Charles politely turned him down. Stryver did not forgive him. He spent much time afterwards denigrating Charles, whom he called "that tutor fellow", and telling everyone how Mrs. Darnay had once set out to "catch" him, but that he'd "refused to be caught". No one believed him except his wife.

When little Lucie was six, the echoes in Soho started to sound more sinister. A great storm was rising in France, one that would sweep all the family in its wake. One hot July evening in 1789, Jarvis arrived for dinner late.

"I began to think I'd have to work all night, there's so much to be done," he said. "There's such unease in Paris that our customers there can't sign their property over to us fast enough."

"That sounds bad," said Charles grimly. "The news from France sounds worse every time I hear it."

Jarvis nodded in sad agreement, then asked, "Where's the doctor?"

"Here," replied Dr. Manette, entering the room.

"Good. I've been unreasonably worried about you all day. You're not going out, I hope?"

"No."

"Good. Where's little Lucie?"

"In bed, of course," replied her mother.

"Good, safe and well. Thank God. Now Lucie," said Jarvis taking her hand, "cheer me up by telling me your theories about the echoing footsteps. I need something to take my mind off France."

Saint Antoine on that same July evening couldn't have been more different from that family scene in London. All day, blades and bayonets had glinted in the sunlight as the people armed themselves with weapons, no matter how crude. No one knew who was responsible, but by the end of the day muskets, gunpowder and other weapons had been distributed freely. What had started as a murmur of discontented voices had risen by evening to a murderous roar.

At the heart of it all was Defarge's shop. The owner, begrimed with gunpowder and sweat, was issuing orders to the men, while his wife took her place at the head of the women. All were armed to their decomposing teeth with knives, axes, sticks, stones and whatever else they could find.

"We're ready!" yelled Defarge. "Friends, patriots – the Bastille!"

There was a mighty roar and, upon hearing that last, detested word, the sea of humans rose and flooded the city. With alarm bells ringing and drums beating, the attack began. The frenzied mob ripped down the stonework of the prison and attacked the guards and anyone else in their way.

Once inside, the cry went up, "The prisoners! The records! The secret cells! The instruments of torture! The prisoners!"

The jailers, or turnkeys as they were known, had been threatened with death if they didn't comply, and led them wherever they wanted. Defarge separated one man from the rest.

"Show me the North Tower, quick!"

"I will, but there's no one there" replied the man.

"What does 105 North Tower mean?" demanded Defarge. "Is it a captive? A cell? Tell me or die!"

"Kill him!" croaked Jacques Three, who'd come to find why Defarge was talking to the jailer rather than killing him.

"It's a cell," answered the terrified man. "I'll show you."

Jacques Three, disappointed Defarge hadn't killed the man outright, went too.

They were led through gloomy vaults, past hideously dark dens and cages where prisoners had been kept. The walls were so thick, and the stairways

and passages so numerous, it seemed impossible anyone had ever got out of there.

The turnkey stopped at a small door and unlocked it, saying, "105 North Tower." The walls of the tiny cell were coated in thick black grime. One of the walls had a metal ring attached to it, where the prisoner had presumably been tied up. Carved next to it were the letters AM.

"Alexander Manette," breathed Defarge. He and Jacques Three searched the room thoroughly, then made the turnkey set fire to it with his torch.

Eventually they found themselves back with the mob, which was now shouting for Defarge to lead them. In its midst was the Bastille's governor, conspicuous in his official uniform. Madame Defarge was beside him, shrieking for her husband to take the man to trial. But before they reached the courts, the crowd suddenly turned and attacked. Within seconds, the governor was dead from a multitude of hacking knives. Madame Defarge put her foot on his head and sliced it clean away from his body with one stroke of her blade. A frenzy of bloodlust began. The trial abandoned, the mob's enemies were massacred on the streets and their remains strung up on lampposts, as a sign of the end of tyranny.

Among the crowd were several who had played no part, too stunned by their sudden freedom to comprehend what was happening all around them. They were the few remaining Bastille prisoners, now free at last – just seven of them in total.

The footsteps echoing through Paris that night

were stained as red as the stones outside Defarge's shop when the winecask had broken. But these new stains were so deep it seemed they'd never be cleaned. Poor Lucie had no idea how those red-stained feet were to entwine themselves with the gentle echoes she often thought she heard in her home.

A week later, Madame Defarge was in the wine-shop. She wore no rose in her hat now; the brotherhood of spies had disappeared from Saint Antoine. There was no more food than before, but the local people had taken on a new character. Everyone had learned how easy it was to crush the life out of another person, and this awful knowledge gave them strength. Sitting beside Madame Defarge was the grocer's wife. Her husband and two children looked half-starved but, despite the lack of food, she'd managed to stay plump and extremely strong. She'd earned the nickname of "The Vengeance".

Defarge rushed into the shop in a state of great excitement. "Does everyone remember Foulon? Who told the famished people they could eat grass, and who we all thought was dead?"

"Of course."

"He's alive and in Paris. He was so scared he organized a mock funeral, but he's been found hiding in the country and dragged back!"

The mood in the shop was electrifying. The Vengeance reached beneath the counter for her drum, on which she beat a rallying cry.

"Patriots," called Defarge, "are we ready?"

In one movement, the people of Saint Antoine had gathered with terrifying cries, lusting for revenge. Foulon – who hadn't cared when their parents, their children, their lovers had died without food. Foulon – who'd said starving babies could eat grass – he was here! Within fifteen minutes, the only people left were those too old, too young or too ill to move. The Defarges and The Vengeance led the crowd to the town hall, where Foulon was being held prisoner. He was dragged out, his hands and feet already tied.

The mob descended, stuffing handfuls of grass into his mouth. The choking tyrant was then hauled to his feet and a rope flung around his neck. This terrified man, once so powerful, was now at the mercy of the people. Ironically, it was his past actions that had turned them into a pack of crazed murderers. They toyed with him, like a cat with its prey, swinging him by the rope as if to hang him, then stopping just before death. He was screaming, begging for mercy – but he'd shown them none. Finally his neck broke. His head was hacked off and placed on a spike, grass lolling hideously from his gaping mouth.

Now Saint Antoine turned its fury on the rest of Paris. Not just on Foulon, who'd abused them, but anyone who got in their way, no matter if they were as poor and starved as they were themselves. By the time the mob returned home, the wailing babies they'd left behind were even hungrier than usual. The miserable shops were besieged by people demanding food that wasn't there. Finally, after sharing what scraps of bad bread could be found, they retired to their beds. In just one week, the inhabitants of Saint Antoine had changed beyond recognition.

A change had also come over the road mender's village. The prison on the crag wasn't as dominant as it had been – there were still soldiers to guard it, but not so many as before, and none of the officers in charge knew if they could trust them anyway.

All around lay ruined countryside, yielding nothing but desolation. Every leaf, blade of grass and ear of grain was as withered and poor as the miserable people and their wretched animals. The aristocrats, who had squeezed every last drop from the land, had run away or disappeared. But the road mender spent little time wondering what had happened to them. His most pressing need was still whether he'd be able to fill his belly that night.

One July afternoon he was approached by a tall, shaggy-haired man, covered in the mud and dust of a great many roads.

"How goes it, Jacques?"

"All well, Jacques," replied the road mender. After a short silence, he asked, "Tonight?"

The stranger nodded. Then he lay down to rest, asking the road mender to wake him later. He'd been walking for two days and nights, and fell asleep very easily. The road mender worked until sunset, then woke the slumbering man. The stranger thanked him and set off in the direction of a hill about two miles away. That night, after a scant supper, the village didn't go to bed as usual. Instead, the people gathered around the fountain. Monsieur Gabelle, chief functionary of the village, grew uneasy; he went out alone onto his rooftop to watch.

As the night grew darker, a strange light appeared in the sky from the direction of the chateau on the hill. The home of the cruel Marquis was on fire. The few servants who'd been left there saddled the horses and rode to safety, calling to Gabelle and the soldiers to help save the chateau. The soldiers looked at one another and shrugged. They did nothing.

All around them, lights were appearing. Thrilled by the burning chateau, the villagers were placing lighted candles in their windows in celebration. Of course very few had their own candles, so a large number were "borrowed" from Gabelle's house.

The chateau burned, flames licking all over its stone faces and the trees around it. Back in the village, the atmosphere grew even more heady. Frightened, Gabelle barred his door and stayed up on his roof all night. He didn't come down until dawn, after the people had gone home.

Many other fires were started that night and a great many of Gabelle's peers were less fortunate than he. When the sun rose, they could be seen hanging across once-peaceful streets where they'd been born and bred, raised only by an accident of employment to a status above that of their fellow men. Likewise, there were many people less fortunate than the road mender and his companions, who were turned upon by more assiduous soldiers and strung up themselves.

Drawn to Destruction

It was August 1792. France had become known throughout the world as a terrible country whose people had changed into wild beasts. There was no longer a royal court: the king and queen were in prison and their courtiers had all fled. After years creating the problems that led to the bloodshed, the aristocrats left as soon as they could, denying any responsibility. In London, they gathered at Tellson's Bank, and it became the first place to hear the latest news from France.

One sweltering afternoon, Jarvis was at his desk, talking to Charles. Despite his now advanced age, Jarvis had been asked to travel to France to restore order at Tellson's in Paris. Charles was adamant he shouldn't go and offered to go instead. But Jarvis wouldn't hear of it; he knew Charles would be in danger there.

"You have no idea, my dear Charles, of the difficulties we're in. God alone knows what dreadful things might happen if the mob seized or destroyed the documents held in our vaults there. And this is a very real fear, you know – Paris could be sacked at any time. I have no choice but to go, sort out the papers, and bring back any I can to England."

"When do you have to leave?"

"Tonight. Don't worry, I'm taking Jerry as a bodyguard."

People kept swarming past the desk, all talking of France. Among them was Mr. Stryver, now even further up the legal ladder and even more full of his own importance. He longed to be an intimate of the aristocratic French, and spent much of his time ingratiating himself with the emigrants by telling them what should be done to the revolutionaries. Charles couldn't stand him.

A clerk approached Jarvis, carrying a dirty, unopened letter. As it was laid on the desk, Charles could see the writing on the envelope: "Very urgent. To the former Marquis Saint Evrémonde, of France. Care of Tellson's Bank, London." Although Dr. Manette knew Charles's true name, he'd begged Charles to keep it secret. Not even Lucie knew.

"I have no idea where he is," Jarvis was telling the clerk. "I've asked every gentleman here and no one has any idea where to find him."

"He's the degenerate nephew of the Marquis who was so cruelly murdered," explained one man. "Happy to say I never knew him!"

"A coward who abandoned his post!" said another.

Stryver surged forward eager to join in.

Then Charles spoke up, "I know him."

"Do you?" asked Stryver. "I'm sorry to hear it! The worst sort of scum, I've been told – left his property and all his precious worldly goods to the butchering mob, when he should have been defending his estate." With that Stryver walked away, satisfied he'd won the affection of all around him (except Charles, who didn't count). Jarvis gave Charles the letter and asked him to deliver it.

Charles read the letter as soon as he was alone. It came from the Abbaye Prison, Paris, and was dated June 21, 1792. It was from Gabelle. It related how he'd been seized by the mob in his village and marched on foot to Paris, then imprisoned on a charge of working for an emigrant. The only way he could be set free was for his employer to appear in court to speak on his behalf. The letter was impassioned and pleading, obviously written by a man in fear for his life.

Charles's mind was made up at once. Gabelle was a good man and a loyal servant. His only "crime" was fidelity to Charles's family. Charles felt responsible – he'd been so eager to renounce his name and social position, he hadn't taken the time to do so legally. Though he no longer felt like an Evrémonde, legally he was still Gabelle's employer.

Jarvis was so brave, an old man yet with so much courage. Charles had to be at least as brave as he was. He'd abandoned his responsibilities and acted like a coward. Now he must return to France to save Gabelle; he would leave the following night. But he couldn't tell anyone, not even Lucie or her father. They would only try to stop him. So he decided to write a letter to be delivered by messenger when he'd already set sail. As soon as he arrived in Paris, Charles could go to Jarvis and together they would free Gabelle, but he knew he couldn't even tell Jarvis yet.

At eight o'clock that evening, Charles returned to Tellson's. "I've delivered the letter and have been asked to give you a reply. Taking a letter is too dangerous for you, but could you remember a verbal reply?"

"Of course," said Jarvis.

"It's for a prisoner in the Abbaye, named Gabelle. Please tell him 'he has received the letter and will come'."

The following day was agony for Charles. He spent a wonderful day with his family and the thought of leaving that night was ripping his heart in two. But he knew he must go. That evening, having pretended to have an engagement, he rode to Dover. Two letters were left with a trusted porter, one for Lucie and one for her father. As he crossed the English Channel, he had no idea how near he was to destruction.

In Secret

That autumn, the journey to Paris was very slow. Bad roads, bad carriages and bad horses had always been the norm, but now there were even more obstacles. Every village, no matter how small, was controlled by "officials" of the Republic. They stopped everyone, demanding to see their papers and cross-questioning them. Their creed was: Liberty, Equality, Fraternity – or Death.

Charles hadn't gone very far before he realized he had no hope of returning to England unless he reached Paris and the new regime declared him a "good citizen". One night, he was asleep at an inn when he was woken by a nervous local official, who told him he was being sent to Paris under an escort. Charles politely declined but a man nearby, wearing a red cap, silenced him with a growl and a threatening gesture with his musket.

"It is as the good patriot says," said the official. "You're an aristocrat and so must pay for an escort."

Charles had no choice. He dressed and set out on horseback with an "escort" of two heavily armed patriots. They were wearing red caps with the tricolore cockade, the symbol of the Republic.

At first he wasn't worried – after all, he'd never harmed anyone – but that evening, when they reached Beauvais, he grew scared. As they stopped at the posting house to show their papers and change horses, a throng of people gathered and several voices shouted, "Down with the emigrant!"

"My friends," Charles called out. "Am I not in France of my own free will?"

"But you choose to live elsewhere, so you're an emigrant! And a cursed aristocrat, too," was the reply.

The postmaster stepped in to protect Charles, saying, "Let him be, he'll be judged in Paris."

"He's a traitor!" shouted another.

Charles swung around. "I am not a traitor!"

"Liar! All emigrants are traitors since the decree!"

Charles turned back to the postmaster and asked, "What decree?"

"It was passed on the 14th."

"The day I left England!"

"Everyone says there'll be more," he added. "There's talk of a law condemning all emigrants to death – but that hasn't happened yet."

Charles and his escort – one of them continually drunk and reckless with his gun – finally reached the walls of Paris. The barrier was closed, but a guard appeared.

"Where are the papers for this prisoner?" he demanded. Struck by the word "prisoner", Charles replied that he journeyed freely and was a French citizen. The guard ignored him, repeating, "Where are the prisoner's papers?"

The drunk escort handed them over, including the letter from Gabelle. The guard looked at Charles with sudden attention, then left for half an hour. All around were people waiting to be let through the barrier, every one wearing the red cap and tricolore cockade.

Eventually, Charles was led into a room.

"Citizen Defarge," said the officer to a man inside, "is this the emigrant Evrémonde?"

"Yes," replied Defarge.

"Your age, Evrémonde?" demanded the guard.

"Thirty-seven."

"Married?"

"Yes."

"Where's your wife?"

"In England."

"You're consigned to the prison of La Force."

"Good God!" exclaimed Charles. "Under what law? For what crime?"

"We have new laws, Evrémonde, and new crimes, since you were last here."

"But I've come here voluntarily in response to the appeal of a fellow countryman…"

"Emigrants have no rights, Evrémonde." The

guard handed Defarge a slip of paper with the words "In secret" written upon it, and Defarge led Charles out of the room. As they walked, he asked in a low voice, "Is it you who married the daughter of Dr. Manette, once a prisoner in the Bastille?"

"Yes," said Charles in surprise.

"My name is Defarge."

"I've heard of you from my wife."

"Why did you come to France?"

"To help a friend. Can you give me help?"

"None."

"But I'm to be buried here in this prison for no reason!"

"People have been buried in worse prisons before."

"But not by me, Citizen Defarge... Please, could you at least tell Jarvis Lorry, at Tellson's Bank, what's happened?"

"I'll do nothing for you," replied Defarge. "My duty is to my country and my people. I've sworn an oath against people like you!"

As they walked, a few people turned to stare, but to see a man in fine clothes going to prison was no more remarkable than seeing a tradesman going to work. They passed an orator telling an excited crowd about the glorious new Republic. It was from him Charles learned that the king was in prison and all foreign ambassadors had left Paris.

At the prison, the door-keeper asked, "How many more d'you think we can take?" but Defarge didn't answer. "In secret, too," the man grumbled, looking at the paper, "as if we weren't already full to bursting!"

Charles was led into a gloomy chamber filled with men, women and children. The women were sitting at a long table, reading, writing, knitting, sewing or embroidering. The men were standing around or pacing up and down. The children were playing. They were all trying to pretend they were safe at home. They rose politely as he was brought in, in the manner of those used to fine society. But despite their attempts at refinement, Charles felt he was in the company of ghosts.

A man stepped forward to welcome him, asking who he was and what had brought him there. Charles replied as well as he could.

"I hope that you are not here in secret?" the man asked.

"Apparently so, though I have no idea what that means," replied Charles.

There was a murmur of commiseration, then Charles was led out of the room and up a stone staircase. He counted the steps as they climbed, in the vain hope that one day he might be able to escape. His solitary cell was blood-chillingly cold and damp.

"Why am I confined alone?"

The jailer shrugged. "How should I know?"

"Can I buy paper and ink?"

"No idea. You'll be visited and told. You can buy your food now, nothing more." And with that, he left.

Charles looked around the cell. There was a chair, a table and a straw mattress. The mattress was crawling with lice.

"I am left, as though I were dead!" he said to himself. "As though these lice were the worms to eat my corpse." He began pacing his cell, working out its size. "Five paces by four and a half, five paces by four and a half..." A little later, a listener could have heard him muttering as he walked, "he made shoes, he made shoes, he made shoes..."

Tellson's Bank was now established in the wing of a large, elegant house in Saint Germain. The house had belonged to a great nobleman, but he'd long since fled, dressed in his own cook's clothes. Readers will remember this nobleman as the lord who'd once required five men just to prepare his hot chocolate.

It was September 3, 1792. Revolutionaries were in charge of the parts of the house that weren't occupied by the bank. Jarvis Lorry was living in the part that was. From his window he could see the courtyard, where the nobleman's carriages had been left to decay. Now there was a new sight to be seen: an enormous grindstone. Jarvis shuddered as he noticed it and lowered the blind to block it out.

"Thank God," he whispered fervently, clasping his hands in prayer, "that no one I love is in this dreadful, dreadful city tonight." Imagine his surprise, then, when moments later, Lucie and her father entered the room. "What are you doing here? What's happened?" he asked, bewildered.

"It's Charles..."

"What about him? He's not here, is he?" asked Jarvis, becoming concerned.

"He's been here three or four days. We didn't know he was coming." Lucie then told Jarvis about Charles's letters and why he'd had to return. "All we can find out is that he's been taken to prison."

Jarvis let out a cry. At the same moment, a commotion broke out in the courtyard below. Dr. Manette moved to the window.

"No!" cried Jarvis, "Don't look out! Come away."

The doctor misread his concern. "It's alright my friend, none of those patriots would harm me. I'm a Bastille prisoner. My old pain has given me a power that brought us here safely, and gained us news of Charles." His hand was back at the blind.

"No! Don't look!" shouted Jarvis in desperation. "Lucie, my dear," he said, putting his arm around her and holding her close, "tell me about Charles. Which prison is he in?"

"La Force," she replied.

Jarvis felt sick inside. "Listen to me, you have to be brave, and you also have to be utterly discreet. Do not leave this place tonight. You must stay here for now. I'm going to take you to a room at the back of the house. You'll be safe, but keep the blinds closed. Your father and I will decide what to do."

Having got Lucie safely out of the way, Jarvis returned and beckoned the doctor to the window. He raised the blind. The grindstone was surrounded by people who'd become so savage you could see it immediately in their faces. The grindstone handle needed two men to move it. As they turned it, their long hair flapped back in the wind and revealed hideously distorted faces of terrible cruelty, stained red by an excess of wine and blood. All around them were more fiends smeared equally red, bringing blood-stained hatchets, knives, bayonets and swords to be sharpened.

His voice broken with emotion, Jarvis whispered, "They are murdering the prisoners. And when their weapons become too blunt for their vile task, they bring them here to sharpen them – and then run back to kill more. If you're really sure about being safe, you have to leave here at once, go to La Force and use whatever influence you have to save Charles from these devils."

The doctor rushed from the room at once and ran to the courtyard. Jarvis heard the cry, "Long live the Bastille prisoner! Help for the Bastille prisoner's kindred in La Force!" Then he saw his friend being lifted high upon the shoulders of the men, the same men who'd so recently been grinding their weapons to kill prisoners. He was carried aloft in the direction of the prison.

Jarvis lowered the blind and hurried to tell Lucie. He was astonished to find Miss Pross – the ever-faithful Miss Pross, who'd once sworn so vehemently never to cross water – and little Lucie with her. All three were worn out with fear and fatigue. Lucie and her daughter were lying miserably on the bed.

As he entered, Lucie sat up. "What's happening outside? What's that awful noise?"

"Hush, don't frighten the child. It's just people using a grindstone in the courtyard," Jarvis whispered. Then they all sat waiting, throughout the night, comforted only by each others' presence.

In the morning, Jarvis crept back and peered from the window. The sun was rising, casting a deep red glow over the courtyard, but the grindstone and the nearby cobbles were stained a far, far deeper red.

A Time
for Waiting

Charles's family wasn't allowed to stay at the bank's premises, so Jarvis found Lucie lodgings to rent nearby. That afternoon, Jarvis heard someone climbing the stairs. It was Defarge. He had come from La Force, carrying a letter in Dr. Manette's hand: *"Charles is safe, but I cannot safely leave this place yet. This man bears a note from Charles to Lucie – please take him to her."* Jarvis joyfully agreed.

In the courtyard were two women, knitting. One was The Vengeance.

"That's your wife, isn't it?" asked Jarvis, pointing to the second woman.

Defarge nodded.

"Does she need to come too?"

"Yes, in the future it may help if she can recognize their faces. It's for their own safety."

Jarvis was struck by Defarge's dull, expressionless manner. He felt deeply uneasy about taking the women to Lucie, but he had no choice.

Jerry, standing guard at Lucie's door, let them in. Lucie was alone and crying. Thrilled by Charles's note, she grasped Defarge's hand in gratitude – a hand that, unknown to her, had inflicted untold horrors only the night before. The note was short:

"Dearest, take courage, I'm well. Your father has influence around me. You cannot answer this. Kiss our child for me."

A grateful Lucie turned to Madame Defarge and kissed her rough hand, but it was pulled away at once. Looking up at her, Lucie was gripped by a sudden terror, as though a shadow had passed over her heart.

"What does your husband say in that note?"

"That my father has influence," replied Lucie nervously.

"Well, let's hope it helps," said Madame Defarge, with a mocking smile.

Jarvis interrupted, "Lucie, these women need to be able to recognize you and little Lucie so they can protect you if necessary."

Lucie called her daughter. Miss Pross, who brought her in, couldn't speak or understand any French, but she looked at the two women, and they looked at her, with mutual dislike. Madame Defarge stared at little Lucie.

"Is this his child?" she asked, still knitting.

"Yes," replied Jarvis, "His only child."

Lucie instinctively drew her daughter close.

"I've seen enough. We can go," said Madame Defarge. Her manner was menacing, Defarge looked nervous and Lucie felt terrified.

She appealed to her, "Please be merciful to my husband, for my daughter's sake."

"The wives and daughters we know have had no mercy shown to them," she replied coldly. "Is it likely one more wife and child would concern us now?"

The Vengeance nodded agreement, and they left.

Defarge followed slowly, looking back sadly at Lucie.

It was four days before Dr. Manette returned. In that short time, 1,100 helpless prisoners were slaughtered. But he didn't tell Lucie this until many years later. She knew only that some prisoners had been killed, but that Charles was safe. The doctor told Jarvis he had passed scenes of carnage on his way to La Force. There he'd found a self-appointed tribunal, before which prisoners were brought and "tried". Some were killed, some released, and some sent back to their cells. One of those in charge was Defarge.

Dr. Manette had identified himself as a former prisoner and pleaded for Charles. His son-in-law had been brought forth, tried and seemed about to be acquitted. Then a secret conference had taken place, and Charles had been returned to his cell. Dr. Manette had no idea what had happened. He was promised Charles would be kept in "safe custody" and could do no more for the moment. He'd then been kept busy tending the sick and wounded.

Jarvis had worried the return to Paris would cause the doctor to relapse, but the opposite had happened. His suffering had turned to knowledge and power. For the first time since being rescued he felt he was of real use to other people. He used his medical training and influence to become "inspecting physician" at La Force, and saw Charles every week, passing messages between him and Lucie. For years Lucie had been the strong one, taking care of her father, but now the roles were reversed.

Months passed and Charles had still not been

brought to trial. Bigger things took precedence – the king and queen were tried, doomed and beheaded. Every day more people arrived in Paris to join the fight for the Republic, and every day more prisoners, most of them entirely innocent of any crime or cruelty, were killed. There was no pause, no time of intervening peace, just slaughter, day after day after day. The Guillotine became a familiar sight – and its sharp blade was always hungry for more victims.

Meanwhile, Charles remained in prison.

A year and three months passed, and every day Lucie feared that Charles would be taken to the Guillotine. The streets were always filled with carts, known as tumbrils, taking prisoners to be beheaded. But Lucie had to be strong, for little Lucie, so she pretended everything was fine and life was the same as it had been in England. It was only when little Lucie was in bed and Lucie was alone with her father that she could cry. Her father would kiss her and say resolutely, "I am sure I can save him. Nothing can happen to him without my knowledge."

A few weeks after Charles had been imprisoned, Dr. Manette had come home with the news that Charles was sometimes able to look out of a small window, at around three in the afternoon. If Lucie stood on the street opposite, he'd see her, though she couldn't see him. So every day Lucie stood there for two hours, between two and four o'clock. If the weather was fine, her daughter went too; otherwise she went alone. It wasn't safe to make any kind of signal, so she just stood still, in all weathers, hoping her husband could see her.

The place where she stood was the corner of a dark, dirty street. There was only one house there, which belonged to a woodcutter. It bore all the marks of a Republican: the tricolore flag, the painted words: "Liberty, Equality, Fraternity, or Death", little decorated pikes and a tiny model of the Guillotine.

The woodcutter (who'd once been a road mender) often saw Lucie, though he told himself she was none of his business. He greeted her in the style that had become law: "Good day, citizeness," to which she must reply, "Good day, citizen." Lucie was unnerved by him, but she knew she had to be friendly. She chatted pleasantly and often gave him money to buy wine.

December 1793 was the bloodiest month so far. One day, amid light snow, Lucie was waiting in her usual place; the woodcutter wasn't at home. Suddenly she heard and saw a howling, singing mob rushing towards her. In the middle was the woodcutter, hand-in-hand with The Vengeance. Lucie hid in the shadows and watched as the throng began dancing to a popular revolutionary song. But what dancing – the movements were so violent they looked like demons dancing in hell. Lucie was terrified.

Eventually the mob passed and she crawled out to find her father, who'd rushed over from the prison. He'd seen the dancing, and knew how she must feel, having felt the same fear the first time he'd seen it, but he comforted her by saying he'd just left Charles climbing to the window. Looking around, he said, "There's no one here, quickly, blow him a kiss." But as she was doing so, they heard footsteps. Both whirled around to see Madame Defarge.

"Good day, citizeness," said the doctor hurriedly.

"Good day, citizen," she replied, and she was gone, casting a malignant shadow over the road ahead.

Dr. Manette took Lucie's arm. "Let's go," he hurried her. "Charles has been summoned for trial tomorrow. We must tell Jarvis."

"For tomorrow!" she repeated with alarm.

"Yes, but don't be afraid, trust me."

"I do," replied Lucie, but she was still afraid. The dancers and Madame Defarge had reminded her how barbaric people had become.

They hurried to Tellson's in search of Jarvis, but who else was visiting him? Not that they saw anyone else, but somebody had to own that riding-coat hanging on the back of the chair, even though Jarvis came out to them alone.

A Knock at
the Door

The dreaded Tribunal of five judges, the public prosecutor and a jury sat every day. That day, 15 prisoners were tried before Charles, and all were condemned to death in just an hour and a half. At last the court heard: "Charles Evrémonde, called Darnay."

Charles looked around the room. Apart from Dr. Manette and Jarvis, it seemed all were armed, both men and women, with knives. Many were eating and drinking as they watched the prisoners prepare to die. Most of the women were knitting. Charles caught sight of the Defarges; they were close to the dock, yet neither looked at him. They just whispered to one another.

Charles was accused of being an emigrant and therefore condemned to die, even though the law had been passed after his return to France. The crowd was calling for him to be beheaded, but the prosecutor rang his bell for silence.

"You've lived in England for many years?"

"Yes."

"Then why d'you say you're not an emigrant?"

"Because I left France of my own free will,

appalled by what I saw as a corrupt, cruel system. I wanted no part of it. I renounced my aristocratic status."

Then Charles gave the name of his two witnesses: Alexandre Manette and Théophile Gabelle. The court cheered at the name of Manette. The court then heard his wife was the daughter of Alexandre Manette, and also French, not English. His case began to seem more hopeful. When asked why he'd returned to France, he explained it had been to help a friend and countryman – not an aristocrat, a servant.

Gabelle himself had just been freed three days before – having been forgotten, if truth be told. He'd only been remembered when he was called to give evidence. But no one alluded to that now, least of all Gabelle, who was just grateful to be free and in possession of his head. He confirmed everything Charles had said. His letter was also produced as evidence.

Dr. Manette was next. He named Charles as his friend, and the faithful husband of his daughter. His trump card was to tell the court that, far from being considered an English aristocrat, Charles had been imprisoned in London and tried as an enemy of the state. This went down very well. Jarvis was then called to give his account of Charles's trial in England. The court was now cheering for Charles and the prosecutor declared him free!

Men, women and children now changed from bloodthirsty beasts back into human beings. All tried to hug and kiss the acquitted man. He was lifted on their shoulders and carried from court. No matter that, even before Charles's supporters had left the room, five more people had been tried, sentenced to death and dragged back to their cells to await the Guillotine. The same people who held Charles on their shoulders would be at the scaffold tomorrow, to watch those five heads roll – but for now they were celebrating.

The doctor ran ahead of the jubilant crowd to tell Lucie, who was waiting ouside their lodgings with Miss Pross and little Lucie. In all the months the family had spent in those rooms, the sounds of happiness and laughter had never been heard. But now they were all talking and laughing at once. Lucie hugged her father and thanked him, still shaking with fear at what might have been. Her father laughed, "Don't tremble – I've saved him!"

They were together at last – though the tumbrils could be heard going past in the streets outside, filled with less fortunate prisoners, and the sound cast a shadow over their happiness. It had become law that the name of every occupant of a house had to be painted above the door. Jerry now added Charles's name.

Lucie kept no servant – partly because she had very little money, but also from fear of employing a spy who could turn against them. So Jerry and Miss Pross did most of the work. That afternoon, they set out on their daily shopping trip, but this time to buy food for a celebratory party. As she was leaving, Miss Pross asked Dr. Manette a question to which she'd been longing to know the answer: "Is there any chance now of our going home?"

"I'm afraid not yet; to leave so soon might put Charles in danger again before we could reach the border."

Miss Pross had to repress a regretful sigh.

Jarvis returned to the bank, leaving Dr. Manette, Lucie, Charles and little Lucie sitting together around the fire. It was a comfortable family scene, with Lucie and Charles talking contentedly, and Dr. Manette telling a fairy story to his granddaughter. Suddenly, Lucie started.

"What was that?" she cried. "I thought I heard footsteps on the stairs!"

Charles and the doctor started to tell her she was imagining things when a heavy blow was struck upon the door.

"Oh father, hide Charles – save him!"

"I've already saved him! Let me answer the door."

He did – and four red-capped men burst into the room.

"Citizen Evrémonde, you are again a prisoner of the Republic!"

"How? On what charge?" Charles asked.

"You're accused and summoned for tomorrow."

"Who has accused him?" cried the doctor. "What's this about?"

One of the redcaps looked sheepish. He wouldn't look at Dr. Manette as he replied, "He's been accused by citizen and citizeness Defarge – and one other..."

"Which other? Who?" demanded Dr. Manette.

"You'll find out tomorrow – at the trial."

Then they arrested Charles and took him back to prison.

A Hand of Cards

Unaware of the turmoil at home, Miss Pross and Jerry had almost finished shopping. The only thing left to buy was wine, to drink to Charles's safe return. As their wine was being measured out, a man who'd been talking with someone in a dark corner got up to leave. He came face to face with Miss Pross, who screamed. Jerry, standing behind her, looked as though he'd seen a ghost. At the sound of the scream, the other customers leaped to their feet.

"Solomon!" cried Miss Pross. "What are you doing here?"

"Don't call me Solomon, you fool!" he hissed, in English, though from his dress he looked exactly like a Frenchman. "Do you want to get me killed?"

"But my dear brother..."

"Shut up! We can't talk here, pay for your wine and come outside. Quickly!"

Miss Pross did as she was told, though she could barely see through her tears to find her money. As they walked to the door, Solomon turned back to the company and, in perfect French, gave them some explanation for the disturbance. Whatever he said, it worked, and they all sat down again.

In the safety of the dark streets, Solomon turned on his sister. "Now, what do you want?" he demanded roughly.

"How can you talk to me like that? How can you be so unkind? I had no idea where you'd gone. I've been so worried about you."

"Well I'm fine – and I don't need you poking your nose in. I knew you were here. I know everything that goes on. I could have contacted you if I'd wanted, but I didn't. I'm respected here. I'm an official. The last thing I need is for them to know I'm English!"

As Miss Pross was struggling to take this in, Jerry spoke. "Tell me one thing," he asked, "is your name Solomon John or John Solomon?"

The man went white. "What d'you mean?" he whispered.

"I've seen you before. You were a witness at the Old Bailey, and you definitely gave your name as John. You didn't use the surname Pross, either. I can't remember what you did use, but I know it had two syllables."

"I don't know what you're talking about..." Solomon started haughtily, when another voice joined in from the shadows.

"Barsad was the name."

It was Sydney Carton.

Sydney explained that he'd arrived the day before. No one knew he was coming and he'd wanted to stay out of Lucie's way until he discovered what, if anything, he could do to help. "I saw you leaving the prison and recognized your face, so I followed you," he told Solomon. "Now, come with us."

Solomon refused – until Sydney threatened to call out the good citizens from the wine shop and tell them Solomon was an English spy.

Sydney and Jerry escorted a relutant Solomon to to Tellson's, while Miss Pross went home. At the bank, they found Jarvis. He seemed perplexed to see Solomon. "I can't work out where I've seen you before," he began.

Sydney enlightened him. "He was John Barsad, an

Old Bailey spy. You saw him at Charles's trial. Turns out he's also Miss Pross's brother, Solomon." Here, Jarvis looked at Solomon with double distaste. Sydney continued, "However I've got more alarming news – Charles has been arrested again. I overheard Solomon here in conversation with a friend, who also works at the prison."

Apalled, everyone turned to look at Solomon, who backed away.

"What's going on?" demanded Jarvis, "I only left Charles at the house two hours ago."

"Ask Solomon," suggested Sydney.

"It's true," stammered Solomon. "He's accused and will appear tomorrow."

"And presumably Dr. Manette's name will free him again?" asked Jarvis.

Solomon shrugged.

Sydney said, "I'm worried. Why didn't the doctor know he'd be arrested again? Why wasn't he told? I'm afraid his influence doesn't extend to this trial. None of it makes sense. Life in this city is like a game of cards – you can win or lose at any time, and the winning hand keeps shifting." Sydney broke off to swallow a glass of brandy – in one gulp – then turned to Solomon. "But I have a very good hand of cards. I have you, a turnkey at the very prison to which Charles has been taken!"

"I can't help you. It's impossible to escape," cried Solomon.

"You won't help? What a pity. You see my hand of cards is this: you were once a spy for the English government. The Republic's greatest enemy! Who's to say you're not still working for them, doing a bit of double-crossing?"

"It's not true!"

"Really? Will the good citizens of Paris believe you? Now, what do you think of my hand? Are you willing to play?"

Solomon was silent. Just one word about his work for the English, not to mention other illegal activities he'd been involved with, and he'd soon be on the other side of a cell door. But the truth was worse even than Sydney knew. More incriminating still, he'd been a spy for the overthrown king of France – he'd spied on Defarge, and now here was Defarge at the forefront of the revolution! He could still remember the shudder that went through him the first time he'd come across Madame Defarge knitting. Now, every day, he saw her read from her knitted register, and he knew the name John Barsad was knitted in there.

Sydney spoke again, "And who was the man I saw you with? I seem to remember his face too..."

"How could you? He's a Frenchman," said Solomon quickly.

"He'd a very strange accent for a Frenchman. I say he's English, disguised as French. I've got it: he's Cly! The other Old Bailey spy."

Jerry suddenly grew very alert.

"Cly's dead," laughed Solomon. "I was there when they put him in his coffin."

At this, Jerry rose up. "Cly is not dead! There may

be a coffin buried under a stone with his name on it, but there's nothing in it but earth and bricks!"

Solomon trembled. "How can you know that?"

"None of your business how; I just do! And I could willingly throttle you, Old Bailey spy!"

A bemused Jarvis and Sydney held Jerry back, wondering themselves how on earth he knew Cly's death had been faked!

"Thank you, Jerry," said Sydney. Then he turned to Solomon again. "Yet another card. You're in league with another English spy. Do you still refuse to play?"

"I've told you, it's impossible to escape."

"When did I talk about anyone escaping? I just want to know how easily you can pass in and out?"

"Whenever I choose."

"Perfect. Come with me into the other room. I have a proposal to make to you, in private."

As they shut the door, Jarvis turned to Jerry. "Tell me, what else have you been besides a messenger?"

Jerry looked embarrassed, but didn't answer.

"I hope you haven't been up to some shady business while hiding behind Tellson's good name. If you have, I warn you, you'll need to find another job."

Jerry appealed to him. "There are two sides to everything, Mr. Lorry. I was just supplying the medical profession."

"I'm shocked at you!" said Jarvis, and turned away.

Jerry spent a long time trying to justify himself. "Please, sir," he pleaded, "keep my secret, for the sake of my son and his mother. I'll find another job, but why not let my son have my place at the bank, so he can take care of his mother?"

After a while, Jarvis found himself agreeing. After all, for all his shady dealings in London, Jerry's conduct in Paris had been that of a faithful servant. But their discussion was cut short by the sudden reappearance of Sydney and Solomon.

"Adieu, John Barsad," said Sydney. "If you stick to our arrangement, I promise you've nothing to fear from me."

As soon as they were alone, Jarvis asked Sydney what he meant.

"That if Charles is found guilty, I can have access to him once."

"That's all?"

"It's all we can do. To do any more would mean Solomon himself would go to the guillotine."

"But it won't save Charles."

"I never said it would. It's all we can do, Jarvis — and don't tell Lucie. I couldn't ensure access for her; it's too dangerous. Don't even tell her I'm here. I'd better not see her."

Jarvis nodded. They sat before the fire and Jarvis cried, silently.

Sydney watched him with pity. "You're a good man and a true friend," he said. "I wish I'd lived a life like yours."

"But you're still young and I'm an old man."

"Yes, but you have the love of a whole family. When you're gone, they'll cry for you and miss you.

I can't say that of anybody. Tell me Jarvis, if in all your years you felt you'd done nothing good or worthwhile, wouldn't you see your life as useless?"

"Yes, I suppose I would."

They stared at the fire in silence for a while.

Eventually Sydney asked, "When are you leaving?"

"My business here's finished. I'd hoped to leave as soon as possible, but I don't want to go without the others."

"Are you able to go?"

"Yes, my papers are in order," Jarvis replied. Then he stood up. "I must go to them. Lucie must be beside herself. Will you be at the trial tomorrow?"

"Yes, but not with you. Barsad will find me a place."

They left together. Jarvis walked to the Manettes's lodgings, while Sydney wandered the streets, deliberately walking routes he knew Lucie would have taken. Eventually he found himself opposite La Force. The woodcutter was outside his house, smoking a pipe. Sydney chatted amiably, though he felt the same revulsion Lucie had felt.

"63 shaved by La Guillotine today!" the man was saying with glee. "Soon we'll be up to 100 a day. You must go and see her in action!"

Sydney resisted the urge to grab the man and beat him, said goodbye politely and walked away.

He kept walking until he found a pharmacist's shop still open. He handed the pharmacist a piece of paper on which he'd written the names of two medicines. The pharmacist looked surprised.

"Be careful, you know what can happen if you take these together?" he warned. "They'll knock you out for hours."

Sydney nodded, paid him and left. Then he walked. All night. He thought about his childhood – he could vividly remember his parents' funerals. He kept remembering the words that had been said at his father's grave: "*I am the resurrection and the life.*" Strange how they should keep coming back into his mind. He repeated them as he walked. All night.

In the morning, he ate a scanty breakfast, then hurried to court. His spy found him a well-concealed place. Sydney noticed how people backed away from Solomon in fear. He could see Jarvis, Dr. Manette – and Lucie. When her husband was brought in, she looked at him with so much love and tenderness that everyone could see the change that came over him. If anyone had been looking at Sydney at the same time, they'd have seen the same change coming over his face. But no one was looking.

The court heard that Charles was a member of a family of tyrants, who'd used their privileges to oppress the people. He'd been recalled to trial because of new evidence. He was openly accused by three people.

"Who accuses him?"

"Ernest Defarge and Therese Defarge."

"And the third?"

"Alexandre Manette."

The court was in uproar.

Dr. Manette leaped to his feet and shouted, "It's a forgery! I would never accuse my own son-in-law!"

"Silence! If the Republic should demand the sacrifice of your daughter herself, you as a good citizen should comply! Now listen to the evidence."

The doctor sat, his lips trembling. Lucie held his arm.

Defarge was called. He was questioned about what had happened when they stormed the Bastille. He described having gone to 105 North Tower. He told how, when they searched the room, he found a piece of paper hidden in a hole in the chimney. "I've had it examined by a handwriting expert," he announced, holding up the paper for all to see. "This is the writing of Alexandre Manette."

The paper was handed to the Public Prosecutor to be read. Everyone's eyes were on Dr. Manette, but he didn't see any of them. All he could see was the piece of paper.

The Letter from North Tower

The paper was read: "I, Alexandre Manette, of sound mind, write this in my prison cell in December 1767. It's written at stolen intervals and I've made a little hole in the chimney to hide it from the jailers. These words are written with difficulty, in scrapings of charcoal and soot mixed with blood. I no longer believe I will be released or rescued, and am writing this only in the hope that one day someone will find it and know the truth about what happened.

"On December 22, 1757, I was walking by the Seine not far from my home. A carriage drove up, very fast, and I heard someone call my name. There were two gentlemen inside, who were so similar I realized they must be twins. They asked if I was Dr. Manette, they'd been to my home and been told I was walking along the river. They said they had an urgent medical case and almost pulled me into the carriage.

"We drove rapidly to a large, solitary house in a neglected park. They rang the door bell and we waited a couple of minutes before it was answered. This angered them, and both men viciously struck the servant for taking too long. I was led to a bedchamber where a beautiful young woman of about twenty was lying on the bed. She had brainfever and her arms had been tied down, to stop her *from injuring herself or anyone else. One of them was tied with a scarf on which I could see an aristocratic coat of arms and the letter 'E'. I discovered later that this was the crest of the Marquis Saint Evrémonde.*

"She'd twisted herself around so she was almost suffocated by the bedclothes. I moved her gently and made sure she could breathe. Suddenly she called out 'My husband, my father, my brother!' then sobbed piteously. This was repeated again and again; the sound of a soul in torment.

" 'How long has she been like this?' I asked one of the haughty brothers.

" 'Since last night.'

" 'Does she have a husband, father and brother?'

" 'She has a brother.'

" 'Is that you?'

" 'No!' he said with great contempt.

"I did all I could to make her comfortable, but I could see she was unlikely to survive. I could also see she was in the early stages of pregnancy.

"After I'd done what I could for her, one of the brothers said carelessly, 'There's another patient.'

"I looked at them with alarm. 'Another emergency?'

" 'Possibly' he replied, disinterested.

I was led to a loft above a stable. Lying on a misshapen bed of hay was a young man of about seventeen, dying from a deep wound. I told him I was a doctor and there to help. I could see he'd been stabbed with a sword. He told me he was the girl's brother. That the two noblemen owned the land on which his family lived, as tenants, with very few rights. One of the brothers had wanted to take his sister: not to marry her, she was of the wrong class, but she was beautiful enough to make him want to keep her for a while. His father had refused and fought for her. The noblemen had then made sure they had no work and no money. Their family was close to starvation and their father died. His daughter, however, married a good man and helped raise her younger brother and sister. She was going to have a baby. But one of the brothers still wanted her for himself. He caught her husband and beat him to death, then kidnapped the wife. He, the brother, had come here armed with a sword to get his sister back. He'd fought with her abductor and been fatally wounded. And here he was, dying, unable to save her.

"Beside him lay an old, broken sword that had once belonged to a soldier. Next to it lay a strong, modern nobleman's sword, stained with blood. I could see how easy it must have been for the aristocrat to win the fight. The boy grabbed my arm so he could raise himself up and address one of the brothers — the other, who'd kidnapped the girl and fatally wounded this boy, had left already.

" 'Marquis,' he said, 'you and your brother are the worst of an evil race. I curse you both!'

"He put his fingers in the wound until they were covered with blood and then drew a cross on his clothing. He did this twice before his strength left him and I laid him down, dead.

"I then returned to his sister. She continued to rave for 26 hours, after which she subsided into a deep faint. She lingered like this for a week, occasionally coming around and talking coherently before the fever took hold again. I tried talking to her, to find out her family name, hoping I'd be able to find her younger sister, now all on her own, and help her. But she wouldn't tell me. All the time the twins hovered, sometimes coming in to see whether she'd died yet and looking irritated that she hadn't. The Marquis, who'd heard what the boy had said to me, always looked at me with grave dislike. I was alone with her when she died.

"When I told the twins of her death, they didn't conceal their pleasure. They congratulated me, and tried to give me gold coins as payment. I declined, politely. They exchanged looks, but said nothing. I was driven home to my wife. The next morning, the coins were left on our doorstep. I hadn't told my wife what had happened; she was pregnant and I didn't want to upset her. Instead, I determined to write to a government official to tell him all I knew. It was unlikely it would ever be brought to court – aristocrats have far too much influence – but I felt that then I would have done all I could.

"On December 31, just after I finished the letter, I was visited by a pretty young woman, who introduced herself as the wife of the Marquis Saint Evrémonde. She didn't know about the woman's death, and wanted to find her and help her. She knew her husband was a bad man, and his brother was even worse. She was desperate to right the wrongs inflicted by their family, in an attempt to free her own child from the hatred attached to his name. She was a good, compassionate woman, miserable in her marriage to a tyrant. Her young son, Charles, who was about two or three years old, clung to her throughout.

"That afternoon, I delivered my letter by hand. Later that evening, my servant boy, Ernest Defarge, showed up a man dressed in black who urged me to come as fast as possible to an emergency. I said goodbye to my wife — who begged me not to go — and left. As soon as we reached the man's carriage, a hand was clasped over my mouth and my arms pinned behind my back. The twins then appeared out of the shadows. The Marquis took out of his pocket the letter I'd written, and burned it to ashes in front of me. Not a word was spoken. I was bundled into the carriage and brought to the Bastille. My living grave. I've not seen my wife, nor the outside world, since. On this last night of 1767, I denounce the family of Evrémonde to the powers of Heaven and Earth, and pray they will be struck down as a cursed family of tyrants."

A terrible sound arose when the reading was finished. The courtroom echoed with howls for the life of the prisoner, that he should be made to pay for the sufferings his ancestors had inflicted. There was barely a dissenting voice in the room, only the cheers and jeers of the crowd. Amid them stood the Manettes and Jarvis, stunned and appealing in vain to the judge.

"Much influence he has, that doctor!" said Madame Defarge, smiling, to The Vengeance. The jury voted unanimously: back to prison and death within twenty-four hours!

Darkness Falls

When the courtroom had emptied and Charles was about to be led away, Lucie called out to his jailers, "Please, please let me hold him, just once!"

Charles looked at her uncertainly, until Barsad gruffly gave permission. The jailers brought Charles over to Lucie, and the two embraced. Then Charles turned to Dr. Manette. The doctor looked as though the life had been drained out of him. He started to apologize, but Charles quietened him. He knew it wasn't the doctor's fault, and apologized himself for everything his father and uncle had done. He admitted he had known of their deeds and had tried to make amends, journeying to France in search of the remaining daughter – but to no avail. This was what had led to him being accused of treason and put on trial at the Old Bailey all those years ago.

As Charles was taken away, the doctor clutched at his hair, as if he would pull it out of his scalp, and gave an anguished shriek. As the door shut behind them, Lucie fainted. Sydney ran over from the dark corner where he'd been hiding, picked her up and carried her to the carriage.

When they arrived back at the Manette's lodgings, Sydney carried Lucie up to her room. Miss Pross and little Lucie came in to help.

The little girl rushed up to him, saying, "I'm so glad you're here, Sydney, I know you'll be able to do something to help Papa!"

He smiled at her and said he'd try. Then he bent down and kissed Lucie's cheek. She was still unconscious, but little Lucie standing next to him heard him whisper, "For one you love."

Then he left the room.

Downstairs, the doctor and Jarvis were talking. Dr. Manette was planning to approach everyone he knew in Paris, to try to save Charles again. But, as Jarvis walked with Sydney to the door, he confessed he didn't believe the doctor could succeed.

"This time, Charles will perish. There is no real hope."

"Yes, he will perish. There is no real hope," echoed Sydney, as he strode out into the night.

Sydney paused in the street, unsure where to go. He'd agreed to meet Jarvis at the bank at nine that evening, but there were several hours before then. "Wouldn't it be a good idea to show my face," he mused, "to let people know what I look like?" He remembered the Defarges had a wine shop and set off for Saint Antoine. On his way he stopped for dinner and, for the first time in many years, drank no strong alcohol. He seemed to have lost his taste for it.

He reached the Defarges' shop at around seven. The only customer was Jacques Three, who was drinking at the counter, talking to the Defarges and The Vengeance. Sydney barely gave them a glance.

He walked in and took a seat. When Madame Defarge asked what he wanted, he requested a small glass of wine. Anyone who knew Sydney would have been surprised to hear him speaking. Normally he spoke French like a native – after all, he'd been a student in Paris – but tonight he struggled with the words and accent like a complete beginner.

Madame Defarge looked at him as he spoke, and surprise registered on her face. As she went to get his wine, she whispered to the others, "He looks just like Evrémonde!"

Defarge, wanting to take a look, took the wine to Sydney and said, "Good evening."

"Pardon?" said Sydney, in a dreadful accent.

"I said, good evening."

"Ah, yes, um, good evening, citizen" replied Sydney, haltingly.

Satisfied the new customer wouldn't be able to understand their conversation, the four continued talking.

"Madame Defarge is right," said Jacques Three. "Why stop here?"

"We must stop somewhere," reasoned Defarge.

"Only at extermination!" snapped his wife. Jacques Three and The Vengeance croaked agreement.

"But the doctor's suffered enough. You saw him when the paper was read," said Defarge.

"Yes, I saw him," replied his wife contemptuously. "And I saw his daughter. In fact, I've seen her a great many times, mostly in the street by the prison, waving to her husband…" She turned on her husband. "Sometimes you make me sick! I think you'd rescue that wretched Evrémonde if you could, just to make your precious doctor happy!"

"No, I wouldn't. But I do think we should stop it here. You have your prisoner. Why do you want the rest of them to suffer?"

Madame Defarge turned to the other two. "I'll tell you why I want to end his miserable race. My husband knows, but he doesn't seem to understand. You remember today, when the paper was read, how the dying boy and woman talked of their younger sister?"

Jacques Three and The Vengeance nodded.

"I am she! That murdered boy was my brother, that abducted woman was my sister. Her unborn child, who died with her, was my little niece or nephew. Now you see why I want the whole Evrémonde family destroyed!" She turned back to Defarge. "So don't tell me to stop! I'll stop when I am ready and not a moment before."

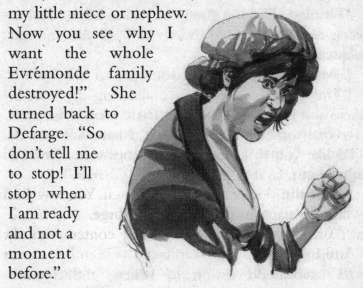

More customers arrived and the conversation ended. Sydney paid for his wine – slowly working out which coins he needed and getting confused – then left the shop.

At nine o'clock, Sydney went to meet Jarvis, but he had barely arrived when the doctor knocked on the door. And as soon as he entered, it was clear all hope was lost. He was muttering helplessly, "Where's my bench? I can't find it. I've been looking everywhere and I can't get on with my work. I must finish those shoes!" Lost, utterly lost! Jarvis helped the doctor to a chair, where he proceeded to sit and shed tears, imagining himself back in prison. Sydney picked up the doctor's coat, which he'd flung to the floor. Out of a pocket fell a piece of paper. Sydney seized and read it.

"Our last chance is gone," he said to Jarvis. "So I'm going to ask you to do exactly as I tell you and not to question why."

Jarvis agreed, grateful for someone to help him.

"This paper is a certificate allowing the doctor, Lucie and little Lucie to leave Paris. I knew he must have one somewhere. Now look, I have one as well – I'd like you to keep it for me until tomorrow. I'd rather not take it when I go to see Charles."

"Why not?"

"I just have a feeling about it. Will you keep it safe for me?"

Jarvis nodded.

"I have good reason to believe the doctor's

certificate will be recalled – and soon. So it's vital you get all the family out of Paris tomorrow. Can you organize transport?"

"Yes."

"Good. I saw the Defarges today. They're plotting to accuse Lucie of communicating with Charles in La Force. I also talked to Barsad, who confirmed a woodcutter is being primed to say he saw Lucie making signals. She, her child and her father are all in grave danger. So you must have a carriage, with all of you inside, ready to leave by two o'clock. Bring it to the door of the prison – I'll be waiting for you inside. Keep my certificate safe. If Lucie and her family stay in Paris, they will be denounced as sympathizers with a Guillotine victim – and you know the penalty for that is death. Do you understand?"

"Yes, I'll have the carriage ready and waiting for you."

"Wait only until my place is filled, then leave at once for England. Promise me that nothing will make you change this plan."

"I promise."

"Good. Remember that any delay, any fuss, could lose several lives. But as long as you trust me, they will be saved."

"I will do as you ask."

They shook hands in friendship. Then, Sydney bade Jarvis "Farewell".

The Footsteps
Die Out Forever

In the Conciergerie prison, 52 doomed prisoners were waiting to die that afternoon. They were all destined for the Guillotine, from the elderly tax-collector, whose riches couldn't save him, to the twenty-year-old seamstress, whose poverty couldn't save her. Charles, alone in his cell, had bought paper and ink, and was writing letters. He wrote a long letter to Lucie telling her he'd known nothing of his family's involvement in her father's plight. He reminded her of the time they'd sat in the garden and he'd told the story about the paper hidden in the Tower of London – this, he realized now, must have reminded Dr. Manette of the paper he had hidden in the Bastille. He knew the doctor must have supposed it had been destroyed with the prison. He also praised his father-in-law for never showing any prejudice towards him, even after Charles had revealed his true identity to him.

He wrote to the doctor in the same vein, and asked him to take care of his wife and child. He then wrote to Jarvis, partly as a friend, and partly to ask him to set his business affairs in order. He didn't once think of writing to Sydney.

Charles had never seen the Guillotine, so he had no idea what to expect – how big it was, how many steps he'd have to climb. He paced his cell, hearing an outside clock chiming hours he'd never hear again. Nine gone for ever. Ten gone for ever. Eleven... Twelve... One.... He'd been told three o'clock was the time he'd be executed, so he supposed they'd come for him at two. Just two more hours until death.

Footsteps. Coming nearer. He could hear them stopping outside his cell. Perhaps they'd come for him early. Then he heard low voices outside, speaking in English. The door opened and in walked Sydney.

Charles couldn't believe his eyes. He asked in concern, "You've not been arrested too?"

"No, but I have a hold over one of the jailers, so he's allowed me in. I come from your wife... I bring a request from her."

"What is it?" entreated Charles.

"It'll seem odd, but she wants you to do exactly as I ask. There's no time to explain. Take off your boots and put on mine. Quickly!"

"Sydney, there's no point trying to escape. It'll just mean you'll be caught as well."

"Have I said anything about escape? Trust me. Just do as I ask. Swap your cravat with mine."

"Sydney, this is madness, I won't let you endanger your life as well!"

"Just do as I ask – for Lucie's sake. Now," he continued, "you need to write a letter."

Charles sat down, picked up the pen and waited.

"I'll dictate," said Sydney, "write it exactly as I speak: 'If you remember the conversation we had so long ago, you'll understand why I'm doing this. I'm sure you remember the words I said; it's not in your nature to forget them'."

Charles looked up as Sydney stopped speaking, and saw him reach inside his breast pocket. "Is that a weapon?" he asked.

"No, it's nothing, keep writing: 'I am thankful the time has come when I can prove that I meant what I said. That I am able to do so will make me happy and it shouldn't make you sad'."

Charles put down the pen. "What's that smell?" he asked suspiciously.

Sydney clasped a rag over Charles's nose and mouth – it was soaked in the two substances he'd bought from the pharmacist. Charles struggled briefly, but was soon insensible on the floor. Sydney quickly dressed himself in the clothes Charles had taken off, tied his hair back with the ribbon Charles had been wearing, and called softly to Solomon.

"You see," Sydney whispered to the spy. "I look just like him. Do you see now why you're not in danger?"

"How do I know you won't give me away later?"

"I can only promise. Now, take him out. I acted weak and faint when you brought me in, so it'll just look as if I've passed out at the shock of seeing my friend in prison. It's up to you. Your life is in your hands now. Help me or die with us. When you get to the carriage, tell Mr. Lorry to give him nothing more restorative than fresh air. We don't want him coming around too soon and ruining the plan. Tell Mr. Lorry to remember the promise he made last night and to drive away at once."

Solomon called for assistance and another jailer arrived. He addressed Sydney as they lifted the insensible Charles from the floor, "Your time's near, Evrémonde."

"I know," came the reply.

Then Charles was carried out. Sydney listened hard, anxious that every sound might suggest he'd been found out. But no; the plan seemed to have worked.

Not long afterwards, Sydney heard footsteps approaching his cell. They had come to take him away. He was led into a large room filled with other prisoners. The room had windows, but it was such a dark winter's day that there was barely any light. Worried he would be discovered, Sydney stood in the shadows, staring fixedly at the ground as the other prisoners talked to one another. Then a young seamstress made her way over to him.

"Citizen Evrémonde, I was with you in La Force. You were so kind to me, I was hoping I could stand with you until they take us to the tumbrils."

Sydney raised his eyes from the ground to look at her and smiled. He saw a sudden doubt in her face and silenced her by bringing a finger to his lips.

"Are you dying for him?" she whispered.

"Yes — and for his wife and child."

"You are so brave!" the seamstress said quietly. "Please, let me hold your hand, I'm so scared and your courage may help me feel less frightened."

Sydney embraced her as though she were his sister. Then they stood, hand-in-hand, waiting for the tumbrils to arrive.

At the same time, a coach arrived at one of the city gates. The passengers' papers were handed to the guard. He looked at them, then peered into the coach.

"Alexandre Manette, which is he?"

Jarvis indicated the doctor, still lost in his own frightened world.

The guard nodded. "And his daughter, Lucie, wife of Evrémonde?"

Jarvis pointed out Lucie, who was sitting holding little Lucie.

"So that is her daughter. And where's Sydney Carton?"

Jarvis pointed to Charles, slumped in the corner of the carriage, still out cold.

"What's wrong with him?"

"He's not in good health," replied Jarvis. "We hope returning to England will revive him."

"So you must be Jarvis Lorry?"

"Yes."

A group of officials circled the coach, peering into the luggage, checking underneath it, staring in through the windows. The local people were also gathering around, curious to gawp at Lucie. A small child was held up by its mother so it could reach its arm into the coach and touch the wife of an aristocrat who'd been sent to the Guillotine. Finally, the guard signed the papers and handed them back to Jarvis. The coach party was free to leave Paris.

Still nervous, scarcely believing her beloved husband could really have escaped, Lucie urged Jarvis to make the driver go faster. But Jarvis refused, insisting that hurrying would only make them look suspicious, so their coach continued on its way at a leisurely pace. All the while, an anxious Lucie and Jarvis stared out of the windows, craning their necks to see if anyone was pursuing them.

While Sydney was awaiting his fate, and Jarvis was talking to the guard at the city gate, Madame Defarge was holding a secret meeting at the woodcutter's house, with The Vengeance and Jacques Three. The woodcutter was standing guard outside.

"My husband's a good man, but he has a weakness with regard to the doctor," began Madame Defarge.

"That's not a sign of a good citizen," sighed Jacques, shaking his head.

Madame Defarge silenced him with a vicious look. "I, on the other hand, believe all Evrémondes must be destroyed," she snapped.

"It would be good to get our hands on the child too, especially with all that golden hair," said Jacques encouragingly. "The people so seldom get the chance to see a child at the Guillotine."

Madame Defarge called the woodcutter inside and questioned him. He swore he'd seen Lucie, her child and the doctor all making signals at the prison window – indeed, he would have sworn to anything Madame Defarge wanted, desperate as he was to keep his head on his shoulders. She was very pleased with his testimony, and told him to meet her at eight o'clock that evening in Saint Antoine, so he could swear his evidence to the jury. Then she let him go, so he could go to find a good place to watch the Guillotine before the crowd grew too big.

That done, Madame Defarge announced she was going to see Lucie at once. She knew Lucie would be unable to hide her grief – and to cry for an executed prisoner was a crime punishable by death.

"Take my knitting," she said to The Vengeance, "and put it on my usual seat. I'll see you there in time to watch Evrémonde's head roll!"

As Madame Defarge walked towards Lucie's house, people shrank from her in fear. Her utterly ruthless manner showed in every purposeful step. She was a strong, muscular woman, with a striking face and not a drop of pity left in her heart. She had a supple way of walking, like a tigress in search of prey.

Hidden in the bodice of her dress was a loaded pistol, and hidden at her waist was a newly sharpened dagger.

At that moment, Miss Pross and Jerry were discussing their own plans for leaving. They'd promised Jarvis they would make their own way from Paris and meet the others at the boat bound for England. They'd watched the coach leave the prison, so they knew who it was that Solomon had brought out. Ever since, they'd been terrified that the switch might be discovered.

Miss Pross was also worried about a second coach leaving from the house in one day: too much activity might invite suspicion. Eventually she decided Jerry should go out and hire a carriage, and that she would meet him at the cathedral. He was extremely nervous and wouldn't leave for talking – and, all the time, Madame Defarge and her loaded pistol were getting closer.

"I want to say, miss," said Jerry, "that if we get back to England alive, I will never again work as a resurrection man. Moreover, I will never again beat my wife or complain of her praying. In fact, I fervently hope she's praying at this very moment and will keep doing so. Promise me you'll tell her this if we make it home?"

Miss Pross almost pushed him out of the door. "I promise that if we ever get out of this godforsaken country, I'll tell your wife everything you've said. Now hurry! I'll meet you in front of the cathedral at three o'clock."

It was twenty past two. Miss Pross was terrified of being alone in the house. She imagined red-capped revolutionaries jumping out from every cupboard and doorway, while nightmare faces peered out at her from under all the beds. So when she looked up from bathing her red eyes in cold water and came face to face with Madame Defarge, she dropped the basin on the floor.

"Where's Evrémonde's wife?" demanded Madame Defarge.

Miss Pross still spoke no French, but she could guess what had been said. Quickly she shut the doors of all the rooms, so it wasn't immediately apparent that no one else was in the house. She knew she had to play for time, or Lucie's coach might be followed and brought back. Madame Defarge and Miss Pross then began a heated argument – though neither of them could understand the other's language. Madame Defarge was determined to search the house, and Miss Pross was equally determined to prevent her. Everywhere the Frenchwoman went, Miss Pross barred her way.

Somehow Madame Defarge must have guessed that her prey had fled because she hurled herself at the doors like a Fury, too fast for Miss Pross to stop her. The Englishwoman, who'd never struck a blow in her life, knew at that moment she would have to fight tooth and nail for her own life, as well as Lucie's. There was one door left to open, one more door before Madame Defarge sent a search party after the

Manettes. She rushed at it, but Miss Pross held her ground, and the two women fought like animals. Miss Pross was naturally strong, but so was Madame Defarge, and they seemed evenly matched. Then, seeing Madame Defarge reach for the dagger at her waist gave Miss Pross a burst of strength. She seized the Frenchwoman and got her arm in a deadlock to stop her from reaching the dagger.

But Madame Defarge's other hand was free and she reached inside her bodice. Miss Pross saw a gleam of metal as the barrel of the gun came up towards her face. Blindly she lashed out with her own free hand, striking the gun as it was about to fire. There was a blinding flash, a thunderous crash and the room was filled with smoke.

Miss Pross was slumped against the door, covered in blood, staring at the body of the revolutionary who lay lifeless at her feet. But Miss Pross had not escaped unscathed; her hair had been dragged out in clumps, her face was covered in scratches, and her dress was torn and stained with the dead woman's blood. Terrified someone would come to investigate the noise of the gunshot, she stood up and grabbed her cloak, hat and veil, thankful that fashion allowed her to conceal the marks of the fight so easily. Then she left the house as fast as she could, looking to all outside glances as she always did, swathed in her veil and cloak. She locked the door and, as she crossed the river, hurled the key into the Seine.

She reached the cathedral a few minutes before three, terrified all the time of being discovered and pursued. When Jerry arrived, she almost leaped into the carriage and urged him to set off at once.

"Is there any disturbance in the street?" she asked nervously.

"No more than usual," he replied.

But Miss Pross didn't seem to hear him. He tried again, but it was soon obvious she couldn't hear a thing. She couldn't even hear the sound of the tumbrils rolling past them in the street. The last sound she would ever hear was the boom of gunpowder that had made her deaf.

Six tumbrils carried the prisoners to the Guillotine. People who lived along the streets were so used to the sight that they barely gave them a glance, though some, who were entertaining visitors, watched from upstairs windows, pointing out the carts like exhibition curators.

On this day, however, the guards were being constantly pestered by people on the street. They all seemed to be asking the same question, because each time the guards pointed wearily towards the same man in the third cart. He stood at the back of the tumbril, his hair tumbling over his face, his head bent to talk to a young woman at his side. His arms were bound, but his hands were free and the young

woman clasped one of them in hers. Solomon Pross was standing on the steps of the church, watching the carts roll past and staring anxiously at the prisoners to see whether he'd been betrayed. When he saw Sydney's face, he relaxed. A man behind him called out, "Down with Evrémonde!" and Solomon timidly told him to hush. The man demanded why.

"He's going to pay the forfeit," replied Solomon, "can't you allow him his final five minutes of peace?"

Surprised, the man fell silent.

At the best seats, right in front of the Guillotine, The Vengeance waited anxiously. She'd placed Madame Defarge's knitting on her usual chair, but her friend hadn't turned up. She couldn't understand it.

"She's never missed a day before!" she exclaimed to her companion. Then, as she saw Evrémonde's tumbril appear, she added peevishly, "And now she's going to miss all the fun! I could cry with vexation and disappointment."

The first tumbril emptied, and then the second. Now it was the turn of the third. The supposed Evrémonde descended. He hadn't once let go of the seamstress's hand. He stood between her and the Guillotine, sparing her the sight of it. They spoke as though they were alone, giving each other comfort and courage. Then they kissed and solemnly blessed one another. He released her hand. She was taken, and he was left alone.

The onlookers counted, "Twenty-two."

"I am the Resurrection and the Life," said Sydney to himself. Then he, too, was led forward.

The onlookers counted, "Twenty-three."

Some of those watching were impressed by the calm of this figure as he walked towards his death. If they had been close enough to hear him speak, they might have been still more impressed by the eloquence of his last words.

As Sydney stepped up to the Guillotine, he spoke his last and noble thought aloud: "It is a far, far better thing I do, than I have ever done; it is a far, far better rest I go to, than I have ever known."

In the streets of Paris that night, whispers abounded about Evrémonde. They said his was the most peaceful face ever seen at the Guillotine – that he looked sublime. Others said he looked as though he could see into the future. If he could, what would he have seen? He would have seen Solomon, The Vengeance, Jacques Three and his fellow jurors, as well as the judges, all perish under their own regime. He would have seen a new Paris, a prosperous and beautiful city, rising from the blood of the old.

He would have seen the family for whom he had sacrificed his life living peacefully in England: Lucie and Charles having a long, fulfilled life together and another son, whom they named Sydney. He would have seen Dr. Manette regaining his mind and growing to be an old man, and Jarvis living for another ten happy years. He would have seen Lucie crying for Sydney Carton every year on the anniversary of his death. And he would have seen Sydney Darnay grow up to become a famous barrister, to have a son of his own, also named Sydney, and one day that son being brought to the very site of the Guillotine so he could see where such a brave man died.

Historic Dates

1770 – Louis, Crown Prince of France, marries Princess Marie-Antoinette of Austria.

1774 – Louis is crowned King Louis XVI of France, but proves very unpopular.

1788 – The harvest in France fails, leading to widespread hunger and a period of unrest known as the "Great Fear", when poor workers robbed and burned aristocrats' houses.

July 14, 1789 – The people of Paris storm the Bastille prison, and destroy it. Revolution spreads through France and many nobles flee abroad.

October 5, 1789 – The king is forced to sign a Declaration of Rights, reducing his powers.

June 20, 1791 – The king tries to escape from Paris, but fails.

August 10, 1792 – Following riots in Paris, the royal palace is stormed and the royal family is imprisoned. Many people who oppose the revolution are put in prison or killed.

September 22, 1792 – France is declared a republic.

January 21, 1793 – Louis XVI is sent to the Guillotine.

October 16, 1793 – Marie Antoinette is sent to the Guillotine.

1793–1794 – A repressive regime operates in Paris; so many are executed that it becomes known as the "Reign of Terror".

1795 – A new constitution gives France a democratic system of government.

About Dickens

Charles Dickens was born in Portsmouth on February 7, 1812, to John and Elizabeth Dickens. His family moved to London two years later, but his childhood was unsettled as his father found it hard to manage money. Sometimes the family was comfortably off, but at other times they struggled to pay their creditors.

In February 1824, John Dickens was imprisoned for not being able to pay his debts. The whole family accompanied him to prison, except for twelve-year-old Charles, who had to leave school, and find a job and a place to live. He worked in a factory which made shoe blacking (liquid polish), pasting labels onto the bottles. He hated the job and felt humiliated by it.

After three months, his father was released and the family returned to a more comfortable life. So Dickens went back to school, but he never forgot his experience of working in the factory and making his way around London alone at such a young age. In his novels, he often writes about the horrors of poverty, and particularly about the exploitation of children.

At the age of fifteen, Dickens started work properly. He got a job in a lawyer's office and studied in the evenings. He taught himself shorthand and became a journalist, reporting on events in the law courts. After a while, he began to publish plays and short stories too. In 1836, he started writing *The Pickwick Papers*, using the pen name, Boz; this would eventually be turned into his first novel. When Boz's identity was discovered by the public in 1837, Dickens's fame as a writer was assured.

From this time on, Dickens wrote novel after novel, all published in weekly parts, and each more popular than the last. Within a few years he was one of the most famous men in Britain, and soon became known throughout the world. *A Tale of Two Cities* appeared in 1859. Among his many other works, the following are some of the most popular: *Oliver Twist* (1837), *Nicholas Nickelby* (1838), *The Olde Curiosity Shop* (1840), *A Christmas Carol* (1843), *David Copperfield* (1849) and *Great Expectations* (1860).

In 1836, Dickens married Catherine Hogarth. Despite his public success, however, his private life was less happy. Although he and his wife had ten children together, their marriage was beset by problems and they eventually separated in 1858.

Dickens was a prolific author; he pushed and pushed himself to keep writing, even when his health was failing and he should have rested. He also worked unceasingly for several charities, some of which he helped found, and gave public readings of his works. He loved doing this, having dreamed when young of being an actor, but his family could see that it exhausted him.

On June 9, 1870, Dickens died aged just fifty-eight. In his will, he asked for a quiet family funeral at his local church in Kent, but Queen Victoria overruled his wishes. She decided that the public would want to take part, and his "quiet family funeral" turned into a huge display of public mourning. Tens of thousands of people lined the funeral route, as his coffin was carried to Westminster Abbey in London. The nation went into a state of mourning rarely seen for anyone except a member of the royal family. He was buried in an area of the Abbey that is dedicated to writers and poets, known as Poets' Corner, and his grave still receives thousands of visitors every year.

The popularity of Charles Dickens continues unabated even today, well over a hundred years after his death. His stories remain in print and have inspired many films, plays and other adaptations. *A Tale of Two Cities* is no exception. The first cinema adaptation of the novel was a silent film, made in 1911. It was so popular that two more silent films were made, in 1917 and 1922. In 1935, MGM made a lavish "talkie" starring three very popular actors of the day: Ronald Colman, Donald Woods and Elizabeth Allan. This was followed in 1958 by a film starring Dirk Bogarde and Dorothy Tutin. *A Tale of Two Cities* was filmed again in 1980 and 1989 (starring Sir John Mills). The story has been dramatised on stage many times, all over the world, and has been turned into a musical play, as well as being adapted for television.

Lucinda Dickens Hawksley, the author of this retelling, is the great-great-great-granddaughter of Charles and Catherine Dickens, descended from their son Henry Fielding Dickens (1849-1933) and his French wife, Marie Roche. Lucinda was born in 1970: exactly one hundred years after the death of Charles Dickens.

Henry was the most successful of the Dickens children; he was a prominent lawyer and was knighted in 1922. One of Henry's grandchildren was the novelist Monica Dickens, who wrote books for adults and children, including the *House At World's End* series.

One of Charles Dickens's former homes, at 48 Doughty Street, London, is now the Dickens House museum. Here, visitors can see the house as it would have looked when the Dickens family lived in it, in the 1830s. In 2002, Lucinda Dickens Hawksley created an exhibition for the museum, all about Charles Dickens's younger daughter, Katey, who was a notable artist.